The Endings Man

The Endings Man

FREDERIC LINDSAY

ISIS

LARGE PRINT

Oxford

First published in Great Britain 2005
by
Allison & Busby Limited

Published in Large Print 2007 by ISIS Publishing Ltd.,
7 Centremead, Osney Mead, Oxford OX2 0ES
by arrangement with
Allison & Busby Limited

British Library Cataloguing in Publication Data
Lindsay, Frederic
 The endings man. – Large print ed.
 1. Novelists – Scotland – Edinburgh – Fiction
 2. Murder – Investigation – Scotland – Edinburgh
 – Fiction
 3. Detective and mystery stories
 4. Large type books
 I. Title
 823.9'14 [F]   0753178 001

ISBN 978-0-7531-7800-3 (hb)
ISBN 978-0-7531-7801-0 (pb)

Printed and bound in Great Britain by
T. J. International Ltd., Padstow, Cornwall

For Ellen

CHAPTER
ONE

He said, "I don't want any of my characters to be cardboard." Worried that was too abrupt, he went on at once, "In a crime story, the reader has to care about the victims. Sure, you can begin with a bang, start with a body, but sooner or later you have to care. Unless it's just a puzzle, of course —"

"And yours are certainly more than that." Alex Dickson was an interviewer who took books seriously. He was a man who made you feel better about yourself, Curle thought.

Relaxing, he continued, "It isn't hard to get a good beginning. Middles are the hard bit. And the ending has to be right. It's the ending that sums up the book, puts it all into some kind of perspective, leaves a good or bad taste in the mouth."

"Jack's Friend. That's how the killer signs his notes to the detective. He's referring to Jack the Ripper, isn't that right?" Dickson, an interviewer who read the books he talked about, nodded encouragingly to indicate he knew the answer but that it would be a good idea to share it with their listeners.

Barclay Curle nodded, then remembered it was radio. "Yes, he's referring to Jack the Ripper, of course.

As far as crime goes, there's only one Jack that matters. Jack the Ripper is the prototype of what later, after the fad in the States for profiling and the invention of Hannibal Lecter, came to be known as the serial killer. In Victorian London he killed, what was it, half a dozen prostitutes?"

"Your murderer has beaten that score. By my count, he's disposed of fourteen women."

"As many as that? To be fair, it is over three books. In Russia, didn't they catch someone who had killed hundreds? Fiction can't keep up with reality nowadays. Never mind, Jack was the first serial killer. Same way, come to think of it, that Sherlock Holmes was the first consulting detective." Leaving aside, it occurred to him, Poe's Dupin; never mind, push on. "Both of them looming out of a London fog, one of those pea-soupers they used to have."

"This murderer of yours, though," Dickson said with the air of a man getting back to the point. "He survived your first two books about him. And you haven't killed him off in this one either — or identified him or had him packed off to jail. Does that mean we can expect another book about Jack's Friend?"

"It's always nice to have the option," Curle said. "Anyway, it would have been wasteful to finish him off."

"Wasteful?"

"A good villain is worth keeping."

"Don't you mean a bad villain?"

Curle laughed. "As bad as they come." He settled back in the seat and then eased forward again in case

2

that put him too far from the microphone. "Writing about him late at night when the house is quiet, I've got up from the desk and gone around checking the doors are locked."

"Did you do that when you wrote the chapter in which he kills the traveller?"

"Traveller? Oh, you mean the guy in the next seat who irritates him by being drunk on the plane."

"Drunk on the plane. Drunk when he gets off it with his new friend Jack. Drunk in the restaurant in Manhattan. In the taxi. In the hotel room. All the way through, in fact, until the moment before his death. It's funny and horrible. There's so much feeling there. Do drunks irritate you like that?"

"I don't kill them." He waited for Dickson's chuckle then said, "I've known a lot of people who drank. I've even been drunk myself." That was all he needed to say. What made him go on? "I wouldn't say my father was a drunk, but I came home a few times to find him sitting in front of the microwave waiting for the news to come on."

Did he need another laugh? Whatever possessed him? It wasn't true, but what humour would there have been in the real reason for the microwave incident? For the last ten years of his life my father had Alzheimer's; and he wasn't in his own house, it was in the kitchen of the Home where he was waited on hand and foot — they wouldn't have let him boil a kettle even if he'd remembered how — paid for by me and my sister, or rather her husband who was generous that way. He could picture the face of the carer who had told them

3

about the old man and the microwave, and the way she'd laughed, showing a wide strip of gum. Too much information. If she ever heard this broadcast, his sister would be offended, but chances were she wouldn't; they didn't get Radio Clyde in Sussex. If she ever did, he'd tell her: haven't you heard? Drunks are funny, drunks are characters, nobody wants to think about old men with their brains addled, or at least I don't. I'm a crime novelist not a peddler of self-pitying slop — I'll leave that to others, plenty of them about, try any bookshop.

"Is there anything of your father in the traveller who gets murdered?" Dickson wondered.

"What? No. Why do you ask that?" The question made no sense to him for a moment. Recovering himself, he saw the connection. "You mean because he's drunk?"

"Oh, it's more than that," the interviewer said. "Only five pages, but you feel you know the man. And you care when he is killed. It comes as a shock. You feel as if it is a man being killed, not a cardboard figure. That's why I wondered if some of that emotion you create might have come, even subconsciously, from memories of your father."

How the hell did I get into this? Curle wondered. "I doubt it," he said.

"Looking at the other side of the equation, your killer, Jack's Friend, seems very real. Is it hard getting into the mind of a killer?"

"Anyone might kill, I think, if the circumstances were right. Call it war, provide a uniform and a clergyman to

4

say bless you, my son, and you can mass produce human killing machines."

"Oh, no," Dickson said. "That's too —"

"Too glib?"

"Not the same. Not what we're talking about. These serial killers provide their own context, they don't need wars."

Curle, who enjoyed an argument, leaned forward. "It's interesting, though. The American military was shocked after the second world war that so few of their soldiers had actually wanted to kill the enemy. They brought in psychologists and set up programmes to get the numbers up. I believe now it's eighty or ninety per cent, something like that. Young men and women primed to kill. Makes you proud of science." At Dickson's frown, added on impulse, "Leaving that aside, in private life I do think almost all of us would be capable of killing. I was bullied at school, bullied by one boy in particular. He made my life a misery. I still think of him sometimes. I don't know what would happen if I met him again."

"You mean you might kill him?" Dickson wondered with a sceptical shake of the head.

"Or roll over again just the way I did all those years ago," Curle heard himself saying. He admitted, "That's what worries me."

Dickson studied him for a moment then said, "Let's get back to the book."

Ten minutes later they were finished. Walking him back out to the parking area in front of the studio, Dickson laughed and said, "Would you believe I've had writers on the show who managed to get the title of their new book into every answer?"

"Don't tell me," Curle said. "I've been told I'm a lousy salesman. It drives my agent up the wall."

CHAPTER
TWO

Curle fingered the card in his pocket. It had come in the morning post and he could still feel the sickness in his stomach at his first sight of the signature. He needed to talk out that odd feeling, but before he could draw the card from his pocket, Jonathan Murray asked, "I take it you got the title in a few times? And what about Doug Kirk? How many times did you manage to mention him?"

Barclay Curle turned his wineglass uneasily. "I'm sure his name came up," he said.

"Came up? Came up?" Murray repeated, pink cheeks flushing with scorn. "He's just your bloody detective. Put it another way, he's your bloody bread and butter."

"And not much more than a corner of a slice from your loaf, Jonah, with a dab of margarine on it."

Murray, Johnny to friends, Jonah to people he'd gone to school with, frowned but in the same instant put a small plump hand over his lips to hide a smirk of pleasure. "You shouldn't believe everything you read in the papers."

Catching the gesture, Curle felt an impulse of affection for the plump little man seated across the

7

lunch table. They had first met more than thirty years ago when Murray had arrived in midterm as a boarder to the school in which Curle was engaged in spending the unhappiest days of his life. Too late to become a friend, since Curle was already isolated in his solitary ghetto as Brian Todd's victim, the plump newcomer had at least remained neutral and even made stray offerings of sympathy. Given the schoolboy need not to be picked out from the herd, it had been as much as Curle could have expected. Even then, he had never been in doubt about the goodness of Jonah Murray's heart. A conviction he'd seen no reason to change since they'd renewed their acquaintance after Murray's return from London ten years previously to set up his own literary agency in Edinburgh.

By that time, Curle had published two novels. The first had done well enough for him to give up working in the library; the second, in which he'd attempted to break new ground, had been a disappointment. When the third one came out three years later, it did even less well and the fourth two years after that had been refused by his then publisher and afterwards by five others. "And they keep the book for months and you have to chase them up even to get a no," he'd complained to Murray. With most people pride had kept him silent about the dreariness of that process, but the casual meeting with someone he'd known at school, at a party to which he'd been almost too depressed to turn up, had opened the floodgates. "I don't think it'll ever see the light of day. When you start, it never occurs to you it could end this way. I'm going to have to look for a job." Murray had offered to read the manuscript. Collected it on the Monday and rung the next day to say, "I'll get it published for you. But you'll have to rewrite it. There's a crime novel in there, heavily disguised at the moment. Why should the old man's death be suicide? If the work he's done for this secret group was so shameful, there would be people who couldn't take the risk of him getting a bad conscience. Suppose he's confided his doubts to the wrong person, an old colleague say. Simple as that, we'd have a murder and be getting somewhere. And you can't get away with vague secret groups any more; go the whole hog, and let it be MI5. And you need a villain; a good public-school type never goes wrong. And this nephew Doug Kirk who stumbles over the body and sets out to find out why his uncle committed suicide — forget about him being a librarian. Make him a policeman; amateur sleuths are out of fashion. Call him a detective inspector and I'll get a series for you." And so he had, in the process adding Curle to his client list.

"And you know the next question," Jonah Murray said, lovingly deconstructing the tower of meat and vegetables in the middle of his plate, "Have you started the new book?"

"Early days yet," Curle muttered.

"You're a lazy bastard. That was the trouble with the first books — too long between them. Crime is a book a year game."

"Five out in five years," Curle said. "When you told me it would have to be one a year, I wasn't at all sure I could do it."

"You looking for sympathy? Next book would make six Doug Kirks and that will finish the second contract. If you don't want another one, you only have to say."

"Doug," Curle said moodily. "Why do all fictional policemen have names like Bob, Jim, Jack?"

"They don't."

"They do in Edinburgh. Monosyllabic names to go with their personalities. Dour buggers. I'd like to break new ground. Why shouldn't I have a Church of Scotland minister as my sleuth?"

"Because you're an atheist?"

"Agnostic," Curle said.

By the time they had finished arguing the contrasting prospects of an updated Father Brown as against a reheated version of Philip Marlowe, the meal was over. They had got up from the table before Curle thought again of the card that had troubled him. As they walked through the restaurant, he took it from his pocket, but as he did a flurry of movement at the corner of his eye turned into a man starting up in his path.

"What a coincidence," the man said, catching him by the arm as he went to step aside. He felt the muscle of his arm tighten under the man's grip as if in protest.

"You don't recognise me, do you?"

Reddy-brown hair, plump cheeks, smooth shaven, the neck thickening and fleshy under the chin, a man who had eaten a lot of good meals in places like this. Three other men at the table, his lunch companions, were looking up in curiosity. And Jonah, belatedly realising, broke stride and turned to see what was going on.

10

"Forget it. Stupid of me." As he spoke, the man released his grip, but said something else as he sat back down with his companions. It might have been, "Another time," but Curle was already moving away and couldn't be sure.

"What was that about?" Jonah asked.

"I'm not sure . . . He seemed to think he knew me."

"Too much wine with the meal."

It was only as they parted company that Curle remembered the card in his pocket, but he didn't feel like calling his friend back specially to show it. That might have seemed to give it too much importance. Drawn to his attention like that, the little man might even find it funny. Best to let it go. He didn't want to seem overly concerned.

CHAPTER
THREE

The card had arrived with a small bundle of others the morning of his lunch with Murray. They had made their appearance, together with a cup of coffee and a poached egg on toast, on a tray carried in by his eight-year-old son.

"Happy birthday!" Kerr said solemnly, waiting as his father propped himself up on two pillows.

Curle held up his cheek to be kissed. "Breakfast in bed. Luxury."

"Because it's your birthday."

"A nice tradition," Curle said.

"You've got cards," Kerr said.

"So I have." He shuffled them. One from Kerr, one from his wife, one from his sister and her husband. From his ageing aunts, three separate cards in three separate envelopes despite the fact they lived together. The seventh one was addressed in a hand he didn't recognise, but was the same unmistakable envelope for an occasion. "Shall I open them?"

"Not ours!"

"You sure?"

"Save them for your presents when we have dinner . . . You are home for dinner?"

"Wouldn't miss it. I could open the others."

"Mum's just getting the car out. Do you want to wait for her?"

Curle caught the hesitation in the question and the faintly anxious look common to the sons and daughters of the unhappily married. It seemed no matter how good a face you put on, it was hard to fool children.

"Let's do that."

"I'll put on my school stuff so we're ready to go."

Curle watched him leave and forked up a triangle of egg and toast. The yolk ran yellow as he cut into it. A good boy, a kind boy, earnest, conscientious, doing well at school, a son to be proud of. The only thing a father with a professional feeling for euphony might hold against him was his name. Kerr had been Liz's father's name and when she had suggested it for their newborn son he had limited his objection to mouthing Kerr Curle and raising an eyebrow. "Very nice," she'd said and, things being as they were, he'd left it at that, shutting his mind to the effects of going through life with a name like a hen clucking, and so from the beginning his relation with his son had as an undertow a sense of guilt.

He heard the car backing out from under the bedroom and then the garage door bang as Liz slammed it down.

A moment later, the boy led his mother into the room.

"We only have a minute," she said. Job sharing, she worked as a pharmacist five mornings and two afternoons a week.

"Dad's going to open his cards," the boy said. "Not ours. The other ones."

She gave them a glance. "From the aunts," she said impatiently. "Same as always."

He opened them one after the other and sat them on his tray. From Chat. From Annie. From May. His three maiden aunts. With love, with love, with love. From his sister, more love.

"There's another one," Kerr said.

"So there is." He turned it in his hand.

"Who's it from?" his wife asked and then abruptly shook her head as if disclaiming the question.

"I've no idea. I don't recognise the writing."

"We'd better get off."

She turned away but the boy hung back curious over the small mystery.

"Wait!" Curle said and putting his forefinger under ripped the flap up, slid out the card and opened it.

As if at a distance, he heard the boy's voice. "Who's it from?"

He shook his head.

"Come on," Liz said, taking the boy by the hand and drawing him away.

"But —"

"Never mind. Daddy doesn't want to show us."

Cursing himself for a fool, he got up and followed, card in hand, but got to the landing just in time to hear the outer door slam shut.

14

CHAPTER
FOUR

After their lunch, he stood on the pavement watching Jonah's taxi pull out into the traffic streaming along Queen Street. Only when it had turned the corner into Hanover Street did he begin to walk back the other way. Secretiveness was a habit he'd grown into over the last eight years.

The wonderful (or terrible) thing was that it had been touch and go whether or not he went to the party where he'd met Ali Fleming. It was being held he had assumed because the hostess wanted to make her individual claim on as many of their circle as she could now that her marriage was officially over. Before the split, he'd been friendly with both of them, but if he had to choose one or the other it was no contest. The husband had just taken a job with a London publisher.

He had made an excuse to get out of the invitation, but when the evening of that day eight years ago arrived he was beyond such petty considerations as cultivating journalists. In the morning, he'd heard the front doorbell as he was shaving and run down to be handed a fat envelope by the postman. The typescript of his fourth novel had come back from the firm that had published numbers two and three. He hadn't paid as much attention as he should have to the sales figures of those books; the advances had been good and he hadn't really expected to get royalties. That, so he had been told, was the way things worked for most writers, and happy to be counted among them at all he hadn't given it much thought. He'd glanced at the letter that lay under the elastic band that went round the typescript. "It is with real regret," the editor had written. He'd met her once on a trip to London, a willowy blonde past her best days. "Let me say, I have no doubt you will find another publisher." Most of the conversation at their lunch that day had consisted of stories of how she had managed to survive successive changes of owner and staff shakeouts; the anecdotes of a self-absorbed survivor and a bad sign that he had been too naïve or inexperienced to take in at the time. Rejected typescript in hand, he'd plodded back upstairs and phoned her, hiding his fury so successfully that their conversation had gone on for quarter of an hour. It ended with her saying, "Thank you for being so understanding." He wished her a lingering death.

After a day on his own by evening he was drunk, still able to walk straight and talk clearly but with all his internal monitors switched off. Why not go to the party? He would probably never have another book in need of a review, good or bad.

As he came in, the crowded room seemed to open a path so that almost the first thing he saw was a woman in the far corner. Her dress clung to her breasts and accentuated the fullness of her bottom, making it jut out like the behind of a black woman. She was white,

16

though, with red hair and the jut of her behind was largely an illusion produced by the way she was standing. By the time he'd worked that out, though, it didn't matter and when the man she was talking to had been sent off on an errand carrying their two glasses he walked over and stood in front of her.

She looked at him expectantly and, as he stood with his mind a blank, began to smile.

"Can you read without moving your lips?" he asked.

"Of course."

"Ah," he said, his voice admirably unslurred. "A woman of above average intelligence."

"You're not very sure of yourself, are you?"

It didn't much matter what they said. Later that night when she took off her shoes, she wasn't so tall.

Eight years later it was still going on, though he'd tried once at least to end it and kept away for almost a fortnight. The familiar building rose five storeys above him and he mounted the steps and pressed the button by her name. After a moment, the heavy bolt swung back and he went inside. The stairs were carpeted, the landings variously ornamented, the first with a little table carrying a vase of flowers, the second by a line of prints showing views of the Castle and the open parkland of the Meadows. As he climbed to the third floor, he opened his coat and fingered the card in his jacket pocket. Liz had stamped off with his son before he had a chance to show it to her. He had balked at showing it to Jonah Murray. Third time lucky; he would show it to Ali.

The door eased back under his knock. She wasn't there, though. She must have opened it and gone back inside, which always annoyed him. Maybe it was her way of punishing him for refusing to accept keys for the street door and the flat. He had told her it was because he didn't want his wife to find them. Why take a risk? he'd said to her. The truth was it would have seemed too much like making a commitment. No doubt she knew that.

She wasn't in the front room, a long high-ceilinged room complete with elaborate cornice and a bay window looking out across the street to one of the private gardens common to the New Town. He went back along the short corridor. The kitchen was empty, but when he looked in her bedroom she was there sitting in front of the angled drawing board. She was a graphic artist.

Without looking round, she said, "I've been wanking for four days." She spoke in a little throaty murmur almost like talking to herself.

He put his hands on her shoulders. "Dangers of working at home."

"And I've got a big job to do."

"Maybe it's not a high sex drive. Maybe you just hate work."

She leaned back against him. "Bastard."

In bed looking up at him as he pushed into her, she said, "Chione."

"Uhh?"

"She was a pretty goddess who thought too much of herself."

He pulled almost out and slid slowly in again.

She made a small contented sound, then went on, "A professor of classics called me that. He was older, almost an old man. But he could last a long time."

He grunted and began pumping back and forward. He started to count backwards from fifty. Somewhere around thirty, she clenched her muscles round him and he came in great shuddering gasps.

"He had a beautiful head of white hair. He called me Chione."

She wasn't even breathing fast.

"Fuck Chione," he said.

"Lots of people must have. It was a popular name with prostitutes in Greece, so he told me."

He eased out and rolled his weight off her. The sun lay on the ceiling as if it had been spread with a knife.

"Before you turned up, I was thinking about him. I imagined he was painting me with radium."

"That's physics, not classics."

"I had to lie still and he painted me. Cunt, ass, tits. I lay glowing in the dark and I could feel the poison seeping into me."

"Christ," he said. "If you'd told me that earlier . . ."

It beat counting to fifty.

"It's all about ritual, you see."

He rolled over and fished in the pocket of his jacket hung over the chair beside the bed. Before he could show her the card, though, the phone rang. She lifted it

19

clear of the stand, gave a grunt, got out of bed and carried it out of the room as she listened.

She came back with two glasses of red wine.

Putting the phone back, she said, "That was the most boring woman in the world. And I've offended her by cutting the call short."

"I wouldn't worry about it."

"At my age you don't find it easy to make new friends, so you hang on to the old ones."

"If we knew that when we were young, we could avoid the bad ones."

"They don't necessarily start out that way, just get worse as they go along."

"It's hard to give up on an old friend. It's like one step nearer the grave."

"Christ, you know how to cheer a girl up."

"What about this then?" He handed her the card.

"This is supposed to cheer me up?" She stared at it, "It's a condolence card." He watched the heavy white card turning in her fingers. "*Thinking of you in your hour of grief?* What the hell? Who's dead?"

"No one. It came in this morning's post. See who it's from."

She turned the open card towards him. "I don't get it."

"*Jack's Friend*. It's signed *Jack's Friend*."

She looked up at him blankly. "You know someone called Jack?"

"Christ," he said bitterly, "I thought you'd read my books."

CHAPTER
FIVE

"Is this all?"

The policeman was disconcertingly tall, four inches at least over six feet, Curle calculated, with spatulate thumbs on big hands, the kind of hands he associated with manual work. He'd been behind his desk when Curle was shown in and without getting up had nodded him unsmilingly towards a chair. He looked to be in his late forties with the beginnings of a drinker's nose and dark stiff-cropped hair shot through with grey. His name was Meldrum.

Responding to the tone as much as the question, Curle said, "I appreciate this might not seem important to you."

He paused, but instead of disclaiming a lack of interest the policeman waited him out in silence.

"I should say," he persisted, "that I didn't ask for — I mean I didn't expect this to be dealt with by an officer of your rank."

"The ACC seems to have felt it appropriate."

Despite the studied lack of expression, Curle took the flat statement of fact as an indication of ill feeling. So that's it, he thought. He resents me for being able to get access to an assistant chief constable; he's got me down as someone who can pull strings and he doesn't like that. ACC Fairbairn had given a talk chaired by Curle at the Crime Writers Association Conference the year it had been held in Edinburgh. He'd spoken of a famous unsolved murder from early in his career and Curle, genuinely moved and impressed, had been warm, maybe even a shade effusive, in his vote of thanks. Afterwards Fairbairn had invited him to visit police HQ and personally shown him round the building from the data-handling suite and interview rooms to the gun range in the basement. As thanks, he'd sent a book, the third in the Doug Kirk series; got a note in return to say that Fairbairn had enjoyed it in the summer on a beach in Corfu; and kept up enough of a desultory acquaintance to feel that he might approach the ACC for help. It was that impulse which had brought him to this meeting with the forbidding figure across the desk. He wondered now if Meldrum had been asked to see him as a kind of chore, a staging post on the way to police officers' Siberia perhaps. He looks a dour bugger, Curle thought, the kind to put backs up — not least that of a smooth politically adept operator like Bob Fairbairn.

"I feel as if I'm being stalked," Curle said.

"Stalking isn't a crime," Meldrum said, "not in Scotland. We deal with it under harassment."

"Whatever it's called, I don't want to be the victim of an obsession. I've been told the temptation for most people is to try to ignore this kind of thing and hope it goes away. But from what I've read, that would be a mistake. If it isn't nipped in the bud chances are it'll get worse. Maybe a lot worse." To his own dismay, he heard a shade of pleading as he finished, "At this stage, a visit from a policeman would probably put a stop to it."

"Well, that's the point, isn't it?" the policeman Meldrum said. "You haven't told me what there is to stop. More than this card, I take it."

Curle opened the envelope that had been sitting on his lap.

"I've mislaid the first one," he said, handing over the letters. "I took it for granted I'd kept it, I keep everything. I'm a hoarder, maybe because I'm a writer. I imagine things might come in useful later on." Stick to the point, he admonished himself. He realised this policeman was making him more nervous than he had felt for a long time. And for no reason, no sensible reason. Maybe it was some kind of professional skill the man had. Must be an asset. I confess, I confess, maybe that was how it worked.

"They're all from the same woman. In the first one she wrote to say that my detective Doug Kirk reminded her of her father. This was just after the second book in the series came out."

"Series?"

"I've done five of them. Five novels." And people buy them, he thought, including fucking policemen, they've told me so. "Murder stories, mysteries, different names for the same thing. Some people call them police procedurals. They all feature the same character, Doug Kirk, an Edinburgh detective. He reminds me of my father, her letter said, even though my father wasn't actually a policeman. And she went on to write in detail of her love life. I put it down as a crank letter, but I was bothered enough to tell my agent. There was something eerie about it."

"Your agent?"

"Jonathan Murray. He's well known. He lives in Edinburgh now."

"And he'll remember this?"

"At the time of the first one, he laughed and said, there's a lot of strange people out there. But I told him about the other letters, I'm sure I did, some of them anyway. He'll remember." He looked at the little pile of sheets. "I'll be quiet and let you read them."

But Meldrum set them down, tapping the edges to stack them neatly. "I'd prefer if you told me about them. What there was in them to bother you."

Curle gathered his thoughts. "Not so much the first one. Maybe that's why I was careless with it. God knows where it's got to. It was the next one that bothered me, the letter that came after the third book. She sent me this extraordinary letter claiming it was about her. This is about my mental problems, she wrote. I didn't like that at all. I'm not brave about these things."

"You were afraid of being sued?"

"No! That never crossed my mind. The book was fiction, for God's sake! I mean, I made it up, all of it. No, it was just that I've always had this feeling that there are people out there that if you're lucky you'll never meet, never get mixed up with them. You must meet them, it's your job. But I don't even mean murderers, it doesn't have to be that extreme. I'd a

24

friend who married a brute; when she went back to her parents, he came round and kicked the kitchen door in. Her father had a heart attack. When I got that letter after the third book, that's how it felt. As if one of those people I never wanted to meet had come into my life." He chewed his lip. "Anonymously."

"What does that mean?"

"It wasn't signed. I'm not sure, maybe the first one was. The others certainly weren't. An Admirer, that's what she called herself."

"And no address?"

Curle shook his head. "No. Maybe the first one had, but it's gone. God, it's so infuriating. You keep a diary?" The policeman looked at him, said nothing. "It's like when you look back at your diary to check a date. The important thing's missing. All you've got is a note about a dental appointment." For God's sake, he thought, pull yourself together. "She sent another two after that, not adding anything new, going over the same ground. I kept them, but I stopped worrying about them. Repetition dulled the impact. But then after the fourth book — you'll see when you read them — another letter came. The book was only in the shops a week, something like that. How did you know? she wrote. I committed this murder you wrote about in your book. You call the girl Sally, she wrote, but you know that wasn't her name. It was a grotesque notion. There were five murders in the book, five of them! Why claim that one? At that point someone else might have laughed. I didn't laugh. It made me feel sick."

"And after that?"

"Same pattern. More letters. More than the time before. Five, is it? Six? They're all there. And then, like before, they stopped. Nothing until I published the fifth book, the one that's just come out. To be honest, when it did, I expected another letter, more madness. Instead, the damned card came. I hadn't expected that."

"You're sure it's from this woman?" Meldrum asked.

As he had done when Fairbairn asked the same question, Curle responded with a mixture of surprise and impatience.

"It must be."

"The condolence card is printed in red ink. These," he glanced down at the top sheet of the letters, "are they all typed?"

"All of them. And the An Admirer signature. There isn't any handwriting to recognise." He'd been through all this with Fairbairn. "And I threw away the envelopes the letters came in. It never occurred to me to keep them. I do have the envelope for the card."

"Which may or may not be from this woman. No envelopes. No handwriting. No return address." Meldrum sat for a moment, then patted the stack of letters. "I'll read them," he said, "but I don't see there's much I can do."

Curle found himself being ushered out. He took a stand at the door and said, "I'll let you know if anything else comes. I just know it's the same woman. The thing is her first letter came after I'd introduced this character called Jack's Friend. And I've kept him in every book since. Readers like a good villain." It struck him how little time he'd been given to explain, how unsatisfactory the interview had been. "Did I say that the Jack in that is Jack the Ripper?"

"If something does come," Meldrum said, "remember to keep the envelope."

CHAPTER
SIX

Curle's first impulse had been to refuse.

"I hate AGMs. Balance sheets I can't read and the risk of being elected to some bloody committee."

"Assuming you're asked," Jonah said. They were having lunch for the second time that week. Not a usual occurrence. He'd been surprised when Jonah had rung to invite him.

"Ye of little faith. I'm the committee-man type. People think of me as solid and sensible."

"I won't say anything about appearances being deceptive. You could always say no."

Curle shook his head and, as an old friend who had a sense of his weaknesses, Jonah didn't pursue it. Instead, he returned to the attack from a different direction. "Napier lays on a decent buffet, I hear. And the wine should be drinkable."

"Why are you so keen on me going?"

"It would do you good. You need to put yourself about a bit more. You can't use work as an excuse. You've hardly started the new book." He frowned. "If you've started it at all."

"It's gestating. I'm taking notes."

Dismissing that with a flap of the hand, Jonah said, "No excuse not to mingle — it's what you do when a new book's on the shelves, get out and make yourself available."

"You're in the wrong business. You should have been a pimp."

"Hemingway said you had to get out of the house; go and see the fights once a year, he said, or you'll finish up alone in a room staring at the wall."

"Look what happened to him."

"Maybe he stopped going."

Whether due to Hemingway or not, Curle overcame his wife's objections to his running in and out of the house by telling her he'd a professional duty to attend that evening's AGM of the Society of Authors in Scotland.

He had been at the Craigton campus of Napier University some time before to do a reading to a group of first-year students. Later he was told the university had one of the highest drop-out rates in the country that year and claimed till the joke grew stale that he was almost sure it had nothing to do with him. He'd forgotten how to get into the building, driven past it and turned before finding the entry off a side street. Tucking the car into the first park, he walked up the drive towards the new building opened only the previous year. A curve of glass bulged from the façade, the lit area beyond showing the tiered blue seats of a lecture room. As he approached, his eye was caught by a notice — SMOKING AREA — marking off a length of raked gravel and some hopefully placed bins. Despite this, the wooden planks that covered the path to the doorway were littered with cigarette butts.

The woman at the reception desk directed him upstairs and he came out on to an open gallery with two long tables carrying glasses of wine and soft drinks. A few people were standing around but there was no sign of Jonah so he crossed a bridge-like structure that moved gently under his feet to the lecture room itself. Inside he checked again before finding a place in an upper row of the blue seats at a comfortable distance from the speakers' table. Waiting, he passed the time by studying the net of broad wooden struts that ran across the walls and roof bracing the shell of the egg-shaped interior.

As people came in, he nodded to familiar faces, usual suspects and some he couldn't put a name to, and fretted over the non-appearance of Jonah. Gloomily, he watched the chairman, secretary and treasurer take their places behind the table, and sank in his seat as the minutes of the last meeting were read. His fears of being elected to a place on the committee were unnecessary. Arms had been twisted beforehand and the nominations were made and seconded without fuss. He was reminded of an old communist telling him how it should be done: "I-nominate-I-second-I-accept-Mr Chairman, and no other bugger gets a look in." When no one took the bait of Any Other Competent Business, he was congratulating himself on it being over when the chairman produced a guest speaker. A stout man, his manner an unattractive combination of diffidence and self-satisfaction, he gave a brief history of Napier, lingering as a highlight on the fact that it had been a hospital for shell shock in the first world war. Two of its patients had later become famous. "That's why," he pointed to one side and the other, "the new halls are called Sassoon and Owens." Apart from that, his talk consisted of the importance of the market in Chinese students.

"Not my idea of what a university should be doing," murmured a plump man called Hale, a writer of love stories, buttonholing him as he tried to make his escape.

Before Curle could respond, Jonah accompanied by another man edged his way along a row of seats into the passage and joined them.

"Where did you get to?" Curle asked.

With a bland smile that wouldn't have been out of place in a sudden onset of deafness, Jonah indicated his companion. "My guest," he said. "He wanted to meet you. He's a fan of your books."

"An admirer," the man said. He was sturdily built with a thick fleshy neck and cheeks that shone as if they had been barber shaven. "I wouldn't claim to be a great reader. I'm an accountant; numbers are more my thing."

Hale said with the slight edge of a writer listening to someone else being praised, "Every man to his trade. You won't have any strong feelings about Owens and Sassoon then?"

"I'm not with you," the man said.

"A forgotten writer who was fond of foxhunting and a minor poet who died in the first world war. This place has named two of its new halls after them."

Jonah waved a hand in protest. "Come on, I think Owens was better than that."

"Because you read him at school," Hale said. "People get exposed to him before their critical faculties are properly developed. A university named after Napier of Merchiston who was a great man; you'd think they could have done better. I expect it's because there was a film about the two of them, holding hands in the hospital to avoid going back to the trenches."

This produced a pause. If Jonah had an answer, he didn't volunteer it. The man with him said at last, "Was it a good film?"

"It was a bloody awful film," Hale said, "and I haven't even seen it."

Jonah looked after him as he went off, swinging meaty hips as if stamping the conquered underfoot.

"Would you believe that man is our Scottish Barbara Cartland?" he wondered. "Maybe that's what makes him so aggressive. All that sugar."

Curle nodded no more than a vague appreciation of the joke for he was studying the stranger trying to place why his face seemed familiar.

Catching his look, the man said with a smile, "You don't remember me?"

"Should I?" And then it came to him, "The other day in the Atrium . . . You wanted to say hello. Is that right?"

"And before that?" the man asked.

Before? Curle looked from the red-headed stranger to Jonah and shook his head.

"I don't seem to have made as much of an impression as you suggested the other day then?"

And some shade in the voice, something about the way as he smiled he sucked in the lower lip as if to bite on it; it was like the wipe of a hand across a steamed mirror to show a face. A face from a lifetime ago.

"Yes," Barclay Curle said, drawing the word out slowly, surprised by the steadiness of his voice, "we were at school together. Isn't that right, Jonah? All three of us."

CHAPTER
SEVEN

I'm a believer that facing our fears is good for us, Jonah
had told him, as justification. But he'd told him
bollocks to that. Idle curiosity, like poking animals with
a stick, would be nearer the mark. Without even a hint
to warn him of what was coming. It was unforgivable. If
I'd told you, Jonah had pointed out, you might not have
come.

There was a thought.

Facing fears wasn't his style.

Until he had physically turned to his left stepping off
Princes Street and into the doorway, he was in doubt as
to whether or not he would keep the appointment.

In the event, he'd misunderstood for it wasn't a
meeting between the two of them: there must have been
forty people in the room. He'd asked for Brian Todd at
reception and been directed into the lift and up to this
room on the third floor of the Club. Not seeing Todd
and not knowing what else to do, he wandered through
the groups around the leather couches until he arrived
at the windows looking down on to the busy night
street and the floodlit outline of the Castle on the hill
opposite blurred in the falling rain.

"Sir?"

At the voice, he turned to find a waiter holding out a tray of glasses. He picked a glass of red wine and went back to staring out of the window. Listening to the murmuring voices at his back, the little spikes of fat chuckling laughter, he felt as if at any moment he might be charged as an impostor and the wine taken from his hand. I'll finish it, he thought, and then I'll get out of here. Even when the murmur of voices stilled and someone began to make a speech, he stayed with his back to the room, for some reason unable to bring himself to turn round. Staring out at the night shapes below, he made out how good the cause was and twice heard the name of Brian Todd, once to applause.

As the speech ended, a voice at his side said, "It's Barclay Curle, isn't it?"

A portly man with a high colour and thinning white hair smiled down at him. He felt his usual surprise and unease at being recognised.

"We met once before," the man said. "It was an event at the Book Festival. I'd published a memoir that year. I remember we became involved in a conversation about crime. You made the point that we both owed our livelihood to it."

A memory stirred. "The bench a more elevated one than the pen?" And with a bloody pension. A High Court judge. McNaughtan, was it?

The judge nodded at the window. "I never tire of that view. Even at night."

"It's a fine view," said Curle neutrally, unlikely to tire of it since he wasn't a member of the Club.

"Were you at the inaugural meeting?"

Meeting? Curle looked at him blankly. Of course, of the good cause. "Brian Todd asked me along this evening."

"Ah, Brian. Well, he's been the moving spirit. Or his firm has. But he's been the one who's taken to do with it. He's been a tower of strength from what I'm told."

". . . He always had plenty of energy."

The judge cocked his head shrewdly. "Have you known him for long?"

"I wouldn't claim to know him well. We were at school together."

"That's a claim in itself. We unpack ourselves to one another at school. The masks haven't formed yet."

Curle shook his head. "People change. Don't you think people change?"

"Fundamentally? I doubt it. You know what the Jesuits say about seven-year-olds?"

Fortunately, they were interrupted before Curle could speculate: yum, yum?

"The very man," the judge exclaimed. "I was just hearing that you two were at school together."

"A long time ago," Brian Todd said. "When we met the other evening, Barclay didn't recognise me."

"But you recognised him?"

"Oh, yes."

"You must have changed more than he has then," the judge offered. "Either that or he left more of an impression on you than you did on him."

"He left an impression," Barclay Curle said.

There must have been something in his tone that made the judge narrow those shrewd eyes.

36

Todd laughed. "Some people," he said, "manage to keep their boyish looks."

In a moment, with a parting pleasantry, he drew Barclay away from the judge. The affair was winding down but still it took ten minutes to get out of the room as the accountant ran a gauntlet of well-wishers. In a quiet room on the first floor, they sat over coffee and looked at one another in silence.

Curle, who didn't take sugar, found himself spooning it in and stirring the cup for something to do.

"You're not in the phone book," Todd said.

"No. We're ex-directory."

"Too many fans calling you?"

"No. It's a long story."

"Aren't stories your thing?"

"I don't feel like telling this one."

Todd leaned forward. "I do like your books," he said, "but that wasn't the only reason for wanting to talk, of course. I heard that interview on the radio. Where you talked about being bullied at school."

"If you're wondering, was I talking about you, the answer's yes."

Todd blinked and sat back. "You can't still be angry with me? I thought in that interview you were just talking for effect. You'd said something of the same sort before. About being bullied at school. In an article in a magazine. My wife read it to me."

"You'd talked to her about me?"

"No, no. She likes detective stories. She'd no idea. To be honest," Todd said, "I'd feel silly saying I was sorry. We're both different people."

"It was a long time ago," Curle agreed. "I wouldn't have been surprised if you'd forgotten it."

"You didn't."

"I was the victim."

"That sounds like self-pity," Todd said and made a face at his own words. "All right, I am sorry. Though the truth is, I don't remember in all that much detail, if you want me to be honest. I doubt if I'd have got in touch at all if it hadn't been for something else in that article you wrote."

"Something else?"

"It was what made my wife read to me. She had an idea it might help. God knows what she was thinking of. The times coincided, maybe that got to her."

"I can't imagine what time you're talking about."

"Eight years ago. Like you, I lost a child eight years ago."

Curle felt as if a hand was squeezing the air out of his lungs. With an effort, he said, "You've got that wrong. Eight years ago, my son was born."

CHAPTER
EIGHT

That had been a wet night too, the night his son was born. He'd phoned the hospital and a nurse had told him nothing would happen till the morning. Later he'd learned that while the bitch was lying to him, his wife had been waving frantically to say he should come in because her pains were starting. She was in the intensive care unit because of high blood pressure and hating every moment of it, not least the attentions of the mad woman from the mental home who wandered around behind the great curve of her belly shaking the drips and smiling down in the night. Nothing till the morning and so he'd gone to that party and met the woman in the red dress and gone home with her, and at some point when they were fucking, the time against the wall in the lobby or the first or second time in the bed, some time around there his son had been born. He'd wakened half across the woman and gingerly unclutched her breast to roll as quietly as a thief out of her bed. At home he'd found the nurse's call on the answerphone — his son had been born at half two in the morning.

Mother and son both well. No deaths that night. It had been six years before that night that their five-year-old daughter Mae had been killed.

After leaving Todd in the Club, he walked up the damp slope of Frederick Street, shining under the lamps, to where he'd left his car almost at the far end of George Street. Finding a parking place in Edinburgh was never easy. The events of Mae's death churned in his mind like dirt from the bottom of a pool. Todd had leaned over the pool, stick in hand, and up it had all come.

He had intended to go home after meeting Todd, but there was no way he could face Liz now, or Kerr either, not with that foulness of dirt swirling around the face of his dead daughter. He drove the car on automatic pilot to the building in which Ali Fleming had her flat, drove past it and parked three streets away. That was one of his precautions. There were others: like not taking a key for her flat, like not phoning her from his house, like not taking her out for meals or to the theatre or at all. That had been the way of things during their relationship. He was a cautious man, and she had accepted it, maybe because there were other men in her life, maybe because of some masochistic streak in her. Eight years, though, was a long time for a woman's patience, whatever streak was in her, and a long enough time for luck to have played some part in their affair going undetected.

That night, with his head full of Mae's death, the luck ran out. He hit the buzzer and the bolt went back. As he climbed the carpeted stair to the third landing, sounds of laughter and voices drifted down to him. In all his visits, he'd never heard anything like it. All these years, he could recall passing anyone on the stairs only a handful of times. He froze, one foot raised, alert as a forest animal. He was turning to go back down when the noise was cut off. He let the silence stretch for a moment and stepped on to the landing.

It was no surprise to find Ali's door, the second on the landing, lying a shade open. Going in, he pushed it shut behind him, but when he went through the flat, living room, dining room, bedroom, sticking his head round the door to check the bathroom, the place was empty. If she had pulled a vanishing trick in front of his eyes, he couldn't have been more puzzled. He went back into the living room and was standing in front of the gas fire when he heard the front door being opened. A moment later, Ali was there, raising her eyebrows at the sight of him and stepping aside to let a young man follow her into the room.

He had a mop of blond hair that fell over his forehead and pale eyebrows plucked into two neat arcs. His name, Ali said, was Bobbie Haskell "from the fourth floor. I can't get the video to work and he's going to have a look at it for me."

"Jack," Curle said, by way of introducing himself. "Jack Brown."

"I can do it another time," the young man said. "I mean since you've got company."

"Nonsense," she said. "Jack won't mind." Curle heard the faint emphasis of her irritation. She went on at once, "How did you get in?"

"Your door was open."

"The outside door, I mean."

"I rang the buzzer."

"You must have pressed the wrong one. I wasn't here. I was upstairs."

"The chap on the fifth floor had us all in for a kind of council of war," the young man said. "We've had bother with the roof."

"You have a Scottish accent," Curle said.

"Yes?"

"And an English name?"

"I don't think of it that way," he said.

"Oh, yes. It's the other way round with journalists in Edinburgh. They have Scottish names, but when you meet them they all have English accents."

"He gets bees in his bonnet," Ali said to the young man. "They don't mean anything."

Barclay felt the smile pull at the corners of his mouth like a snarl.

"Everybody gets those," he said, watching her as if they were alone. "For a while with you, it was friends. I remember last New Year you made a resolution to find friends who were less boring than an unexpurgated religious tract. It made me smile at the time. Later it made me realise how discontented you were." He acknowledged the young man's presence. "It's what happens to women when they get near forty."

As quickly as that, they were at war. Not even the sight of Haskell swinging his face like a spectator at a tennis match applied the brake. It was only when he'd left, shown out at last by Ali, that Curle began to cool down.

"What took you so long?" he asked as she came back.

"What are you on about now?"

"You should have got rid of the little bastard right away."

"He's as tall as you are!" And before he could react to the stupid inconsequentiality of that, she blurted, "Maybe I wanted him here as protection."

"Protection? Protection from what, for Christ's sake?"

"From you. In case you hit me."

He stared at her then sank down into a chair.

"That's not my style. I'm not your bloody professor."

In bed later, he said, "If I had hit you, you'd have liked it, wouldn't you?"

"Not for real. For real's different. I can't imagine what made you so angry."

He put an arm across to hide his eyes and said nothing. It felt as if only a moment passed, but it also felt like wakening so perhaps for a time he slept.

She was speaking in a soft reflective murmur. "I was in a shop, a little shop, a very small space, this man tries to come in, he has a pack on his back, no room, I can see there's no room for him. As I tried to squeeze out his bulk pressed me back over the counter. It was horrible."

He took the arm away and turned his head to look at her.

"When was this?"

"No when at all. It was a dream."

A dream. Why tell him her dreams? He wasn't her psychiatrist. Anyway, it was so unlike her usual confidences that he was disappointed.

After a time, he said, "At least the little bastard doesn't know my name."

". . . Jack," she said. "Shouldn't it have been John? Isn't that what prostitutes call their clients?"

"Jack will do."

"Hmmm."

"What? What?"

"Bobbie Haskell works in a bookshop."

"Oh . . . fuck."

CHAPTER
NINE

In a reaction towards the uxorious, Curle took his wife and son out for the afternoon. Naturally, it turned out badly. For one thing, although it was her day off, it was a schoolday and Liz disapproved on principle. No sooner had they left Edinburgh than the sunshine, which had put the idea into his head in the first place, ebbed away as the islands on the Forth sank into a mist and chopping waves on the estuary indicated a rising wind.

"Yellowcraigs to North Berwick," Liz said grimly. "I don't think so."

A walk along the beach had been her suggestion. For a stubborn instant, he felt like insisting they do it, but then had an image of them head down as the wind scoured the beach up to sandpaper their faces.

"I know," he turned the car inland, "we'll go and see Jane Carlyle's house." Speaking firmly into the silence, he said, "It's in Haddington. Twenty minutes or so will take us there. I've always meant to visit it."

He filled the journey with an account for Kerr's sake of who Thomas Carlyle was and why he had been a great man. Had been? Has-been? he wondered as he talked. Who reads him now? He tried to remember what he could about Jane. Great letter writer. Sharp wit. Not particularly happy: being a great man's wife wasn't easy. Desperately mourned by Thomas after her death, guilt as much as anything.

It was a nice little market town, with a main street of undistinguished shops.

Getting out of the car, as they stepped into the beginning of a drizzle, he promised, "Look, there's a café. We'll get afternoon tea after we've seen the house."

There was a sign like an inn sign above the pend. He pushed back the white gate that lay half open and they walked down the narrow lane. On the blank gable end of the first house there was a plate: JANE WELSH BAILLIE. It said she'd lived in that house, that she had been Thomas Carlyle's wife and gone to live in London but come back to be buried in Haddington. Better than being buried in Haddington while you were alive, he thought. The gate into the yard at the back of the house, though, was marked "private". They went on down the narrow lane. At the end, there was an arch and another sign.

The house was shut, not for lunch or a half-day, but seasonally.

"We'll come back in April," Liz said neutrally. But added, "That'll be something to look forward to."

As they walked back, he took a little jump to peep over the wall and saw a tree with apples on the grass underneath. It was a tall cramped house with long narrow windows in a line on the first floor. In each window dirty cream shutters were drawn behind the glass.

In the café he asked for tea, coffee and a Coke. On impulse, he ordered a slab of gateau for Kerr, who deserved to have something out of the trip. When he asked Liz if she wanted one, she grunted and looked out of the window. They had gone down steps into the café so that what she saw was people's legs and the hems of their coats as they splashed past in the rain. They sipped at their drinks and watched Kerr eating the cake, cutting into it with the edge of his fork and putting chunks in his mouth.

When they were finished, he led them back to where he'd spotted the butcher's shop as they drove in. Colin Peat's. He'd read about it in one of the local papers. "It's got game pies and good meat sourced to the farm. We could get something for dinner."

"Are you home tonight?" his wife asked.

"Of course I am!"

"I have to know," she said. "So I know what to get."

When they came out, he took the plastic bag with the steak pie and the venison sausages from her and carried it close against his side to protect it from the rain. While they had been in the shop, the weather had got much worse so that they were soaked before they got to the car.

CHAPTER
TEN

Fuelled by government warnings, premonitions of atrocity had become a background to everyday life, like the heart's pulse you could never again take for granted after the first faltering. In only the last month, this endemic uneasiness had imperceptibly sharpened as if, by some instinct, the heads of grazing animals had lifted to sniff the wind.

Too fancy, Curle thought as he contemplated the words on the monitor screen, I'm writing a detective story not *War* and fucking *Peace*. He took a mouthful of coffee, long gone cold, and tried again.

Some kind of terrorist threat seemed to have been around for ever. This time, though, the evidence was overwhelming. No one doubted some great atrocity was imminent. Fortunately, so much Prozac had leaked from Londoners' piss into the drinking water that the city remained admirably calm.

Toilet jokes. Was that supposed to be an improvement? At least no one could accuse it of being fancy. Had Tolstoy ever written a toilet joke?

48

He hit TOOLS and WORD COUNT and studied the dismal total. By contract he was obliged to deliver the manuscript of the novel in three months' time. A bit of mental arithmetic confirmed that at this rate of progress he should be finished in two and half years.

Have to work harder, he thought, and got up and wandered about. He looked out of the window at the back garden and the back gardens of his neighbours. If the view had been of mountains, he was pretty sure he would work better. Or one of the sea, or of the Forth estuary with its road bridge, rail bridge, tankers going up and down to the terminal at Grangemouth.

He picked up the cup and went down to the kitchen, stepping lightly as a thief on the treads of the stairs. In the hall he stood listening until the roar of the Dyson vacuum started up reassuringly in the front room. Moving quietly past the closed door, he went into the kitchen where he boiled a cupful of water, made instant coffee and negotiated the return journey without mishap.

He didn't have an office in the city to go to; he worked at home. Most writers worked at home. Some worked in a hut at the bottom of the garden. John Byrne worked in a hut. Maybe that was why he was so prolific: to take his mind off the cold.

Curle worked in what had been a bedroom. He closed its door behind him and put the coffee down beside the computer. There were four bedrooms upstairs. One was for Liz and him, one for Kerr, one that he had lined with bookcases was kept for guests. Which left this one. The smallest one. With a computer table and a case of reference books, two office chairs, a desk. Which about filled it. Maybe if he had space to walk about, he'd work better. Maybe not.

In the middle of the room, he stretched his arms wide as if to push back the walls. Working at home could drive you crazy.

Back at the window, he noticed that last night's high wind had torn loose a strip of felt from the roof of the garden hut. No one could blame him if he went down and fixed it, even if he was supposed to be working. He hung suspended between options until after a while an image of his father came unbidden out of the past. He was standing on the lawn, standing beside Curle's mother, and it must have been summer and a party for there were lots of people and the sun was shining. His father with his light cream summer suit and his false face, his professorial smiling face, false as a mask. Like him, his father had been an adulterer and he had hated him for it.

Finally he sat down at the computer again, read over what he had written. Shrank the page and brought up solitaire. None of the games worked out. When he remembered his coffee and took a mouthful, it was cold. It was a relief when the phone rang.

He listened to the voice and said, "No, of course, I remember you."

Meldrum. The policeman.

CHAPTER
ELEVEN

Her name was Martha Tilman and she lived at the top of a hill in the Border town of Peebles.

"You want to go now?" he'd asked in surprise when Meldrum phoned.

"Why not?"

Leave the cold coffee behind. Get out of the house. Why not?

"What age is she?" Curle asked in the car.

"What age would you want her to be?" Meldrum responded.

And what kind of answer was that? Perhaps he didn't know; perhaps he didn't like being questioned; perhaps he couldn't help himself from testing, probing, needing to find out. It was what policemen did after all, and it seemed to Curle that Meldrum was one of those men defined by their job. Assuming he had a private life at all, it was hard to imagine what it might be. A glance to the side gave him a glimpse of the raw-boned profile, big nose, long chin, thin mouth, giving nothing away. The hands surrounding the steering wheel were thick fingered, old scars white on the back of the nearer, hands shaped by grasping tools, a workman's hands.

"Just curious," Curle said. "I never thought you'd find her."

"Why did you ask me then?" Meldrum wondered and then shook his head. "Of course, you didn't. You asked Fairbairn. And where did you do that? For a bet, not at his office. Nothing official, since you didn't really think we could find her. Did you happen to run across Fairbairn at some function? Some kind of dinner maybe, eh?"

"Some kind of function," Curle said.

"Don't tell me. It came up in the conversation. Made a good story. And you thought that was the end of it. But then Fairbairn decided to wag his willie and show you how high an assistant chief constable could pee."

Curle kept his peace, and they were in Peebles Main Street before Meldrum said, "I didn't find her."

"Who did?"

"Nearly there."

And Curle had to content himself with that for an answer as they wound up the hill and came to a stop at the last house, two storeys of new brick behind a wide stretch of lawn.

The man who opened the door was in his middle years, about fifty perhaps, with close-cropped iron-grey hair. As Meldrum introduced them he nodded and gestured them inside. He pointed them to a door and as they went in turned back into the hall, listening all the while to the mobile phone he held clamped against his ear.

They stood looking at one another in silence.

"Private call apparently," Curle said.

Meldrum dismissed that with a look.

Irritated, Curle offered a volley of questions, "Who is he? Why are we here? Is the woman here?"

Meldrum surprised him by saying, "Sorry. His name's Tilman. Joe Tilman. He's by way of being a millionaire. Or he was until the bottom fell out of his business, one of those dot.com things. He's the husband." After a pause, he finished, "Like I said, I didn't find her. He came to us."

The room they'd been shown into was a kind of snug, four comfortable chairs, a coffee table, one of the new televisions with a screen that served as a mirror, glass cabinets with books and sculptures made out of white driftwood and lumps of burled walnut. As the minutes passed, Curle read the titles behind the glass of the nearest cabinet: *Wainwright In Scotland, National Geographic Expeditions Atlas, Britain's Highest Peaks, White Death, October On Everest, South Col, The Munros, The Game Of Ghosts, Antartica, Storms Of Silence*. He recognised the name of the writer of the last book. Joe Simpson. A climber who'd crawled off a mountain with a broken leg.

He turned at the sound of the door being opened. Meldrum was looking at a photograph framed on the wall, hands behind his back in the at ease position.

Tilman came in, sliding the mobile into the pocket of his shirt. He glanced at Meldrum then focused his attention on Curle.

"I take it you're the one who made the complaint?"

Curle, who'd been expecting some apology however perfunctory for keeping them waiting, couldn't find an answer to that. After a moment, he confined himself to a nod.

"You can forget it. You won't have any more trouble from Martha. I hope you'll take my word for that." And as he finished, he half turned as if to lead them out of the room again to the front door.

There was an oddly compelling quality to the gesture, the assumption of a man accustomed to being given what he wanted. Thinking about it later, Curle had the embarrassing suspicion that if he had been on his own he would have followed meekly into the hall to find himself immediately afterwards on the front step with the door being closed in his face. Meldrum, however, turning from the photograph, took one long stride and was folding his length into the chair on the other side of the fireplace without waiting to be invited. Tilman frowned in something like disbelief. Suspended between them, Curle resolved his discomfort by going to the other chair by the fireside. As he sat, he took in the photograph framed on the wall above him. It showed Tilman and another man with between them two blonde sharp-featured women. The two women linked one another and their male companions by an arm around the waist. Each man draped a possessive arm across the shoulder of the woman beside him. All four offered broad smiles to the camera. The second man was unmistakably Assistant Chief Constable Fairbairn. He saw that Meldrum was watching him. Had the policeman deliberately left him this chair hoping that he would notice the photograph?

He saw that Tilman was also watching him.

"Bob Fairbairn is married to my wife's sister," Tilman said.

Tilman and Fairbairn. There was a theory that you could connect any two people on the planet in six steps. Scotland was a small world. Call it four.

"Can we speak to your wife?" Meldrum asked.

"No."

Meldrum raised his brows at the abrupt negative.

"That wasn't part of the bargain," Tilman said.

"Whatever you've been told, I might decide it is necessary to talk to her."

In the pause that followed, Curle had the impression that Tilman took account of Meldrum, actually saw him, for the first time. He showed no response to Meldrum's tone, but went to the remaining chair in front of the fireplace, leaning back with his hands relaxed on its thickly padded arms. Like that, attentive and alert, he seemed suddenly formidable to Curle; of course, he thought, he's getting ready to negotiate. Making deals is what he does.

"As I explained to Bob — Bob Fairbairn," he said, "my wife has been getting more unwell for the last year or so." Looking at Curle, he added, "She sent you letters, isn't that right?"

Curle nodded. "For more than a year, though. It must be more than three years since the first one came."

Tilman nodded. "I know the dates. I've read them."

Shocked, Curle glanced at Meldrum. Had those letters been given to Fairbairn? Had Fairbairn chosen to show them around? It was outrageous.

Tilman seemed to allow himself a moment to appreciate the effect he had created before he began an explanation.

"My wife was admitted to a private nursing home last week. Florid, you know that word? Her doctors used it. Her delusions were florid. So then I was on my own. It took a few days for it to occur to me that respecting her privacy was no help to her, not by that stage. I decided to have a look through her study, that's what she calls it; it's just a room where she can be by herself. I found a diary in a drawer of her desk. I read bits of it, but I couldn't see how they would be of any help to her doctors. The drawer hadn't even been locked. I was ready to put it back when I saw she'd written a couple of words inside the back cover. Her mother's maiden name. The name of a holiday cottage we have." He shook his head with a mixture of disbelief and what could have been contempt, but might have been pity. "It's what people do apparently. I knew at once what they must be. Passwords. I used them to open files on her computer. There were reviews of your books, newspaper articles, that kind of stuff, and the letters. The letters she'd written to you. Forty or fifty of them."

"That can't be right," Curle said. "Nine or ten. There were only nine or ten."

"Then she wrote more than she sent," Tilman said.

Meldrum intervened. "Have you taken them to her doctors?"

"Not yet. I'll have to think about that."

56

"But you took them to the Assistant Chief Constable?"

"Not the way you mean. His wife was worried about her sister. I needed to talk to somebody. I told them the latest from the clinic and that led on to how I'd found these letters. I'd hardly started when Bob jumped up and said, 'You've solved a mystery'. He was full of apologies for mixing the police up in it, called himself all kinds of a fool. It was his idea that I should see Mr Curle and put his mind at rest. For Martha's sake, that's what I decided to do."

"I see, and the easiest way to put you in touch with Mr Curle was to ask me to deal with it," Meldrum said.

Curle wonder whether Tilman was conscious of the dryness of Meldrum's tone, or if he sensed it himself only because of that earlier interview at which he had been made aware of the policeman's resentment. A touchy bastard, he thought, who doesn't like being treated as an errand boy. By this point, Curle badly wanted to put an end to the proceedings. In retrospect, he felt uncomfortable about having got so worked up over a handful of letters from an unfortunate woman. That overreaction had led to what he now felt as an intrusion into a private grief. As it happened, he was disinclined, not the most useful trait for a writer, to get involved in the messiness of other people's emotions.

While he was shaping a graceful speech, however, vowing to forget the whole wretched business, Meldrum began again. "It is the case, though, that one of the letters sent to Mr Curle claimed to describe a murder. I saw that one myself."

Tilman, presumably still in negotiating mode, didn't react.

It was an incensed Curle who blurted, "A murder that took place only in the pages of one of my books!"

"A piece of fiction, that was certainly my impression," Tilman said, smiling at Curle, "though I don't know how accurate her account was. I'm afraid I haven't read any of your books."

And Curle almost offered the little self-deprecating remark about "joining the great majority" that he produced in such situations.

He was saved from this by Meldrum asking, "In the letter I saw, your wife doesn't name the person she claims to have murdered. Does she in any of the letters she didn't send?"

"Why would you want to know?" Tilman wondered. He spoke quietly, but his right hand that had lain relaxed on the chair arm suddenly clenched. If he was angered, though, that was the only sign he gave.

"If we had the name of this person, it gives something that can be checked."

"The victim she imagines wasn't a woman. It was a man. She talks about a friend of ours. And no, he wasn't murdered. So no need to check."

Curle the peacemaker found himself smiling and nodding, but when Meldrum waited in silence, Tilman went on, "He's dead. Of natural causes."

"What would they be?"

"Would cancer of the testicles be natural enough for you? He was best man at our wedding. It occurs to me as late as this that my wife might always have been a

58

little in love with him. Or maybe it's just a coincidence that those letters of hers about murder were written just after his death. Does that cover whatever it is you wanted to know?"

The woman in his book, Curle remembered, had an affair with a neighbour, both of them married, and she'd killed him because he'd fallen too much in love with her and wanted to tell the world. The playfulness of reversing the usual roles played by the sexes had pleased him. Queen Kong. Ms Hyde. Cancer of the testicles. Punishment for adultery.

He was on his feet.

"I've had enough of this. There was no need for me to come here. All that stuff about the letters, it's all forgotten. As far as I'm concerned, all forgotten."

Negotiation concluded.

They rode back to Edinburgh in silence. He stared straight ahead all the way, not risking a glance at his companion. Time enough later, he thought, to try to work out what Meldrum had thought he was doing, what had possessed him, what had been going on. However irrationally, for the moment he felt endangered and just wanted the journey to be over. Weakly he muttered some kind of conventional parting as he got out of the car, but the policeman drove off without a word.

CHAPTER
TWELVE

It came as a shock to Curle to realise that even Jonah Murray, who'd been there, didn't understand what being bullied by Brian Todd had meant to him. He'd been thirteen when it began and it had lasted for only eighteen months: too old, it might be natural to assume, to be deeply marked by a suffering that had lasted for such a limited time. When he thought of that assumption, though, he recalled how on two or three occasions, into his twenties, brooding over the memory of Todd had turned into a calculation as to how long that dark cloud had hung physically over his existence and how the answer always brought a reaction of disbelief. Only eighteen months! When he came across one or another popularisation of Einstein, he'd had no difficulty in accepting the idea that time was relative.

One day he'd come home in such despair that he had tried to tell his father, that weak pleasant man, what was going on. It had taken an effort even to begin but his father had seemed to be listening, gathering his son down beside him where he sat slack in the big chair. The story had been painfully hard to put into words for he could not help feeling that the fault was his, and the guilt made him ashamed. He might not have managed at all if it had not been for the protective weight of his father's arm laid reassuringly across his shoulder. At last he'd come stumbling to a finish, and sat staring at the picture of his mother that had been brought down from the bedroom. The silence stretched as he waited for a verdict until he wondered if what he had confessed was too shameful to be worth a response; but when he summoned the courage to look up he saw that his father had fallen asleep, mouth open and just then dribbling a first snore.

Around that time, his grandmother had begun to question him as to how often his father came home early from the office, and in a roundabout fashion that soon became insistent and open as to whether or not he had been drinking. He had lied and later would wonder whether something might have been done if he had become her willing spy. As he grew older, however, he encountered other men in the process of falling apart and there didn't ever seem much chance of stopping any of them. Fortunately, it had taken another eight years before his father went bankrupt so that by the time it happened he was finished with university and no longer dependent.

His life had gone awry when his mother died. Todd had paid him no attention before her death. A shark can detect minute dilutions of blood in the water. The bully smells unhappiness.

And now, aided by Jonah, Todd had come back into his life. Over a couple of weeks, there he was, at a dinner given by an acquaintance, at the theatre, at a private view at the Scottish Gallery.

On the last Tuesday of the month, then, it was no surprise to see him among a group of people drinking wine in a room of the National Library while they waited for the reading to begin.

It didn't help that his approach was that of an old friend.

"All prepared? I wouldn't have the nerve myself." His proprietary smile passed from Curle to the librarian who was going to introduce him. "I'd rather climb a mountain in a snowstorm than make a speech in public."

"You know what happened to Joe Simpson," Curle said inconsequentially.

"Came off the mountain with a broken leg," the librarian said. "Wrote a book about it. Did a lot of public speaking after that."

Todd looked at them blankly. *Not a mountaineer; a conclusion from which Curle drew an obscure satisfaction.*

"I thought you weren't interested in books."

"It's true I don't have a lot of time for fiction," Todd said. "There's so much else to do. But when Jonah told me you were reading from the latest masterpiece, I couldn't resist coming along." He cast a glance towards the entrance. "I thought he'd be here by now. The three of us were at school together," he explained to the librarian.

Aware that the librarian, as much as himself, would reserve the term "masterpiece" for a very few books indeed and none of them his, Curle drained the glass of wine he'd been given and reached for another. Five minutes later, Jonah arrived and ten minutes after that was registering mild alarm as he watched Curle put away two more glasses.

It was Curle's opinion that no one could get drunk on wine. It was true that in the year after their first child was born Liz and he, lacking a babysitter, would get a bottle of wine as a Saturday night treat and get from it a buzz of happiness. But then little Mae died held across his knees and wine lost its power to help him unwind. All the same, five glasses before doing his turn, if he'd thought about it that was hardly professional. When it came to it, though, he read as well as ever, he felt that to be true, and answered the gently leading questions of the librarian deftly enough. The trouble, such as it was, arrived with the questions from the audience. Even then, it wasn't that he was drunk, for he wasn't, not in the slightest. The difficulty was that the wine had taken the edge off the tension he usually felt about performing in public, a tension that typically translated into a feeling of responsive gratitude as he made his connection with the people in front of him. Deprived of that, he suffered the unfamiliar sensation of being bored. "At one time, you wrote poetry for some of the small magazines. Do you still write poetry?" "I gave up the sin of committing poetry some time ago." Laughter. Why were they laughing? It was no more than the truth. "How do you write?" With great fucking difficulty. But the questioner went on: "I mean, are you very disciplined? Do you keep regular hours?" You could always count on one fucking idiot to ask that. Why did they ask it? Who cared? Were they looking for tips? Climbing Parnassus without tears. Parnassus my arse. How old-fashioned could you get? More like: the beginners' guide to making a supplementary shilling. To that stock question, he'd a stock answer: giving an honest account of the way he wrote irregularly, afflicted with procrastination, but thinking of the book all the time at the back of his mind. Now, bored with the truth as much as the question, he firmed his jaw and lied in his teeth, "I get up at seven, have a coffee, a black coffee," nice afterthought, "and work through till two o'clock when I break for a plate of soup." He thought about saying vegetable soup but lost his nerve, and after that hurried through to the end of his working day without pulling the long bow too far, a trick he left to bigger artists. The librarian asked hopefully if there were no more questions. A hand waved. With dismay, Curle saw that it was attached to Brian Todd. "I was wondering," he asked, "do you ever base any of your characters on real people?" He had an effective projection, cushioned on a full lungful of air, without a trace of nerves, with that deeper timbre that gives a man's voice authority. It wasn't a voice that would have any difficulty in commanding a room, so why claim he couldn't speak in public? On automatic pilot, Curle made the usual joke about the law of libel and trotted out the anecdote about how Simenon as a protest had published his autobiography with all the bits left blank to show how many threats he'd had of being sued. When he stopped, the librarian took his chance and it was over, leaving nothing to do but sign a few books.

64

That finished, he would have made for home but was gathered up by the sociable Jonah and added to a group consisting of Todd and a young man who said something flattering but didn't take the trouble to introduce himself. The night was cold so they didn't venture far. As he walked, Curle was struck by desire for Ali Fleming, whom he hadn't visited in almost a fortnight. The two in front were laughing, the young man beside him said something and he made some sort of reply, all of it blurred by images of her breasts, the curve of her arse, the intricate familiar mystery of her cunt under his hand. Get away as soon as I can, he thought.

In the pub, he tried to buy the drinks, not wanting to stay for a second round, but Todd was before him and brought a pint with a whisky beside it though he'd asked for a half pint only.

"Those admirable work habits of yours," Jonah said, settling back on the bench and blowing his nose. "It's a wonder you haven't written ten times as much."

For some reason as he drank his whisky, it seemed that the story of Grogan would be a suitable riposte to that. It was the tale of a young man who was a whore for the repartee and had no fear of being interviewed by a Dublin wit. Came the moment when the wit asked was he the front end of an ass, was he the back end of an ass, why then he must be no end of an ass. The audience laughed and any other man would have been discomfited. Not Grogan, however. Taking a pace back he looked the wit up and down before responding, Fuck you!

Possibly because he got it slightly muddled in the middle, this story did not go down as well as Curle might have hoped. As he pondered this, the young man appeared with a fresh round, imitating Todd in fetching for the writer, that creative spirit, a whisky as well as a pint, though the others seemed content with just a beer.

As he settled down again, he said to Jonah as if in response to an earlier question, "I've always worked with books. I started with Thins. I'd left before they went into administration, though."

"A good bookshop as bookshops go," Jonah said, "and as bookshops go, it went."

"Nothing stays the same," Curle pronounced gloomily.

He tasted the whisky and decided it was crap. Maybe the young guy hadn't much money. But why buy whisky at all if you weren't going to buy a malt? He hadn't asked him to buy a whisky. He watched the young man push a lock of blond hair back and decided that he disliked him a good deal. He'd pushed himself in, a pest, an intruder, a nuisance, an irrelevance. While coming to this conclusion, following the habit of a child trained never to leave his plate uncleared, he finished the whisky and started on his pint to take the taste away.

Todd, who'd been sitting with the young man also in his sights, suddenly said, "I was talking to a client from St Andrews about his tax return. He told me there was a biologist in the University there studying flies."

"Fruit flies," Jonah said, encyclopaedic as ever. "Use them for genetics."

"No. Ordinary flies, dance flies he called them, out in the fields. Know what they found? They found that males that tried to bribe females with insects didn't do any better than ones that offered them bits of twig. And they got a grant to do it!" He laughed. "To prove that women are stupid!"

And then two voices spoke at once.

Jonah said, "Or that men are bastards!"

And the young man turned to Curle with a wide white smile. "I imagine Ali would have something to say to that!"

As Curle recognised Bobbie Haskell "from the fourth floor", Ali Fleming's upstairs neighbour, he stood up so abruptly that he bumped the glass carried by a man passing behind his chair. Not stopping to apologise, or make the customary placatory offer to buy him another one, he fled.

CHAPTER
THIRTEEN

"Never mix the grape and the barley," Jonah said, buttoning up his coat against the searching wind.

"What are you following me out for?" Curle asked ungraciously. "Stay and finish your drink."

He began to walk down the hill towards Princes Street. Why hadn't he recognised the bloody man? That night in Ali's flat he'd done his best to ignore him, of course. Not a face or personality you'd remember.

"Was it something he said?" Jonah asked, catching up.

"Who?"

"It looked like he said something that upset you. Who was he anyway? I didn't catch his name."

"I thought you were the one who'd come across him somewhere and invited him to join us."

"Not me. I thought you knew him."

"No," Curle said, trying to put the whole absurdity of the idea into one word.

"Maybe Todd knew him."

The possibility horrified Curle. "No," he said again. "I'm sure he didn't."

"A Velcro man then," Jonah said. "One of those people that come along and stick to you. Never mind, if

Todd didn't know him before, now's his chance." He gave a little snort of laughter.

Curle grunted. Oddly enough, what he was missing at that moment was the chance to talk over what had happened. If it had been anything else, Jonah and he would have been going along with their heads together, weighing, assessing, teasing it out, more often than not processing it into gossip or joking about its possibilities for the making of fiction. He was a private man but not a particularly self-contained one. The keeping of a secret didn't come naturally to him, and more and more recently he had found the need to conceal his relations with Ali Fleming somehow chilling, like a shadow unexpectedly cast across spontaneity. A shadow cast over small as much as large things, like now when Jonah was assuming they were both on their way home. Should he go home?

They began to walk along Princes Street, the Castle looming on their left above shadowy spaces of grass and trees. When they were almost at the west end of the street, Jonah said, "There's a taxi. You take it. I'll get the next one."

There were plenty of them about, the city was generous with its licences, and Curle flagged down the first one.

He gave his address and waved to Jonah who, nearly at the corner, could hardly miss noticing if the taxi didn't turn left into Lothian Road. The opposite direction, as it happened, to that in which Ali Fleming's apartment lay. Jonah, in his turn, would be crossing Princes Street and going back the way they'd come.

Curle sat back in the seat and watched the shopfronts go by. All he had to do was let the cab take him home. He leaned forward and tapped on the glass. What was it Wilde had said? I can resist everything but temptation.

From the beginning, this visit was different. He was surprised after climbing the stairs to see Ali waiting in her doorway to greet him. It seemed she had been roused out of bed for she was in a pyjama top and shorts and her feet were bare. She smiled at him, "I needed cheering up tonight." He could smell the muskiness of her body warm from the blankets. As he went in past her, the bedroom was on his left. He turned right into the front room. There was a scatter of magazines on the couch and a bottle of whisky and a glass on the low table. In the grate, the artificial coals of the unlit gas fire piled in lumps of black and grey.

"What are you doing?" she asked following him. "It's cold in here. I was feeling lousy so I had a whisky and an early night. I've been in bed since eight o'clock."

He no longer knew why he had come. After a moment, she sat in a chair and gathered her feet under her.

"Aren't you going to take your coat off?"

"I don't think so."

"You'll be hot in bed." As he stood abstracted, her smile flickered and faded.

"It's no good," he said. "It's no good any more."

"Do I have a say in this?"

"It's no good for you."

70

"And you're only thinking of me. Of course you are."
She looked down at her hands in her lap. "Would you
like me to beg?"

"You've too much pride for that."

"What did I ever do or say that gave you that idea?"

He made a chopping gesture of impatience. "Don't
tell me I'm the only one in your life."

"How many are there? Have I always had someone?
All the time you've known me? If you thought that, why
did you never say?"

Had he always believed she had other lovers? Not
always. Perhaps lately. He shrugged. Men are cowards,
they always say they'll phone. Where had he heard that?

"I could have written you a letter," he said. "But you
deserve more than that."

Her laugh took him by surprise. He had heard her
laugh before, at one time very often, but it had never
sounded like this.

"A letter? You must be joking. If you go, you've taken
care to leave nothing behind."

"I won't be back," he said. "I've taken up enough of
your life."

All the way down the stairs, he expected to hear her
door opening, her voice calling after him.

The night had turned colder. It wasn't true that you
couldn't be alone in a city. The pavement ahead of him
was deserted. He needed a taxi to take him home. He
turned up his collar against the wind. Last winter on a
night as cold as this, he had been about to cross the
Meadows with Liz, when a young man had begun to
walk alongside them. He was wearing an anorak,

trainers, no gloves on his hands. He spoke in a low confidential tone, not coaxing, or wheedling, just describing how he lived and that he would be sleeping rough that night. The three of them walked side by side with the dark expanses of grass on either side, and Curle waited for the boy, for he didn't seem much more than a boy, to ask them for money. It occurred to him that if he could get at his wallet, he could extract a note by feel and even be sure that it was a pound and not twenty for he ranked his money so that he wouldn't make a mistake of that kind. He could fold it in his hand and simply pass it over to the boy as they parted, saving him the awkwardness of having to ask, for it seemed to him that the boy was hungry for company almost more than anything. When they came to the end of the path, however, the boy wished them a good night and turned away. It happened quickly, but not so quickly that Curle couldn't have said, here's something for you; but by then it would have meant taking out his wallet and he was too cautious for that. Afterwards naturally he was ashamed, but what good was that?

Head huddled into his collar, Curle made his way up the hill under the burden of his guilt, which was real however self-indulgent.

CHAPTER
FOURTEEN

He woke in the morning smiling and lay watching a fragment of a cobweb in the corner of the ceiling sway in an air current trying to work out why he was happy. He felt carefree, not a worry in the world. All my bills paid, he thought, I can look anyone in the eye. Who knows, I may even finish the book in time. Stranger things had happened.

He got up and drank a glass of water, washed his face, stuck his head under the tap and towelled himself dry. He put on his dressing gown and stuck his feet in slippers then came out on to the landing. Not a sound. He'd had broken sleeps for a long time, wakening at five, lying awake, getting up tired and heavy eyed. Was it possible he'd overslept? He felt refreshed and ready for anything. In the kitchen, he found it was almost ten. Liz would be at work, Kerr at school. To his surprise he was disappointed not to see his wife this morning. He thought about that as he made toast and coffee. With a kind of disbelief he contemplated the possibility of making a new start. Things had gone wrong, but it didn't have to be that way. I'll get my life back on track, he thought.

It was in that spirit that he went to see ACC Fairbairn.

"I have a meeting at twelve," Fairbairn said glancing at his watch. "That gives me quarter of an hour free."

He had a phone for the outside world on his desk and, for some reason, a pen and pencil set, perhaps some kind of award or gift, and a silver-framed picture of his wife, whom Curle recognised from the photograph he'd seen in Joe Tilman's house.

"I shouldn't have come without an appointment," Curle said. "I came on impulse. I didn't really expect you'd be able to see me."

"Not for long, I'm afraid."

"I wanted to thank you for helping me with the anonymous letters." Watching Fairbairn tense slightly, he knew he'd begun in the wrong way. Hurrying on, he said, "I appreciated it very much; you didn't have to. I wanted to say that. Of course, once I'd learned who sent them, the background to it, a sad story, I regretted ever raising the matter. It's the end of it as far as I'm concerned." He paused. "I just wanted to say that too."

At ease now, Fairbairn sat back in his seat and nodded. "I'm told she's being helped. We just have to hope for the best."

Curle hitched himself to the edge of his chair and they stood up more or less together.

As Fairbairn walked him to the door, he asked, "When can we expect another book?"

"By the end of this year," Curle said, and added superstitiously, "God willing."

"I'll look forward to it."

74

They were shaking hands when Curle said, "I should thank DI Meldrum, too. It was good of him to come with me."

Fairbairn closed the door he'd just opened.

"Meldrum was with you?"

Surprised by his tone, Curle confined himself to a nod.

Fairbairn shook his head slowly. His expression was that of a man silently rehearsing a vocabulary of swear words.

"He ran me down to Peebles," Curle explained. "I was glad of the offer. It saved me the trouble of trying to find the house."

"It's not difficult to find," Fairbairn said grimly.

"He wasn't supposed to take me?" Curle guessed.

"My fault," Fairbairn said. "I gave him the information because he was working on this problem you had with the anonymous letters. He's the type you have to call off. Otherwise, once he's got his teeth in something . . . I should have phoned you myself, but having spoken to him it seemed tidier to get him to round it off. And this is all he was supposed to do. Give you a ring and ask you to contact Joe Tilman."

Without perhaps giving it enough thought, Curle said, "He struck me as someone who wouldn't much like being used as a messenger."

Fairbairn seemed to rehearse silently a darker range of curses. "That's not the way we work. If I give an order — But I'll be told I didn't spell it out clearly enough. If there was a shade of ambiguity — That's how the Meldrums of this world —" He broke off as another thought struck him. "Did he take you there and wait outside?"

"No. He came in with me."

"No need to say any more. No doubt, I'll hear about it." From Tilman, Curle thought. At once, though, Fairbairn asked, "Did he just sit and listen?"

Uneasy by now, Curle tried to keep his tone as neutral as possible. "He asked some questions." The last thing he wanted was to get embroiled in a matter of police discipline.

As if reading his mind, Fairbairn said, "He's a difficult man. His career's more or less blocked — not by me! — something that happened years ago. Past time probably that he left the force, but that's not easy to do if it's all you're good at. I sometimes wonder if he's trying to get himself kicked out."

Unconsciously, did he mean? As one himself, Curle was deeply sceptical of amateur psychologists. He mumbled what might have passed more or less for an agreement of sorts, which brought Fairbairn to a halt. He reopened the door, offered his hand again and said, "Best ignore all that, eh? I know I can count on your discretion." He laughed. "Doesn't matter since you'll never see him again."

Curle was in the lift before he allowed himself a smile. A writer's discretion, he thought, there's an oxymoron.

CHAPTER
FIFTEEN

On a balance of probabilities, the best estimate was that Ali Fleming had died in the last hours of the previous day. Somewhere around the time on the following morning when Curle was leaving the office of ACC Fairbairn, the stillness of the dead woman's flat was being disturbed by the persistent ringing of the bell on the street door. The owner of the small agency where she worked had stopped by on his way to lunch. It was by chance that the design she had been working on was urgently needed. At a loss, sure that she would have phoned to explain if she was ill, her employer came back to try again just after five in the afternoon. By coincidence, Bobbie Haskell arrived home to find him there and, having heard of his anxiety, used his key to let them both in from the street. Repeated knocking, followed by banging, on the door of her flat brought no response.

Haskell repeated the performance twice that evening with the same lack of response. The following morning he delayed going to work until he could phone the agency where Ali had worked, using the number the owner had left him. Learning that she still hadn't appeared, he went down and beat such a tattoo on her door that her downstairs neighbour, a widow in her late fifties, came up to enquire about the disturbance. She volunteered the information that when she had been sitting up in bed reading, not the previous night but the one before, she had been startled by "thumping" noises from upstairs. This confidence led to a long conference about what they might do, which ended only when Haskell, torn about being so late for work, trailed off indecisively to the bookshop. It was the widow, Mrs Eva Johanson, who having spent much of the day pondering her anxiety made the call to the police, which led to the discovery of the body that evening. Soon after, the process was initiated which brought to the building and filled the rooms of the flat with scene of crime officers for pictures, swabs, fingerprints, and a medical examiner and detectives under the senior officer available when the call came.

It was then almost sixty hours after Ali Fleming's death, just before noon on the Friday morning, before Curle was summoned from his study by his wife.

"There's a policeman wanting to speak to you," Liz told him.

He pushed to roll back his chair from the computer and stared at her.

"A policeman?" Like most people, he associated a visit from a policeman with news of some accident or mishap. "It's not Kerr?" As he spoke his son's name, his stomach sank in fear.

"Oh, God," she said, as if the idea had just forced itself upon her.

When he followed her into the front room and saw that the taller of the two men waiting for them was Meldrum, his first reaction was relief. They weren't here about Kerr. This was followed by something like embarrassment for it occurred to him that perhaps Meldrum had been ordered to apologise to him. He even had time in the hurry of his thoughts to consider that the second policeman might be there as a witness to sharpen the penance or to make sure it had been undertaken at all.

As if they hadn't met, Meldrum introduced himself and then his companion, "DS McGuigan."

Still caught in the improbable scenario of an apology, Curle asked, "It is just me you want to see?"

It was Liz's turn to look relieved.

After she had left the room, Meldrum asked, "Do you know a woman called Alexina Fleming?"

In his surprise, Curle failed to recognise the name in this unfamiliar form. He shook his head.

"We've been given to understand," Meldrum said, "that you've been in the habit of visiting her at her flat in Royal Circus."

Ali?

He shook his head again. Wouldn't it be foolish to admit anything until he knew what this was about?

"You're saying that you don't know Alexina Fleming?"

"No."

He waited for the same question to be asked again. It was what policemen did; hammer away at the same question. This time I'll tell the truth, he thought.

"Would you mind telling me where you were on Tuesday evening?"

To his horror his mind went blank. "Tuesday?"

"Tuesday evening."

Of course. He knew where he'd been. He told himself to calm down; it was ridiculous to feel such relief. "On Tuesday evening I had a talk to give at the National Library. That's on George the Fourth Bridge," he explained.

"I know where it is. Can you give me times?"

"The reading started just after half past seven. The event finished — I can't give you an exact time — before half past nine."

"What happened then?"

"I went home. No — I went with some people for a drink."

"Could you give their names?"

"Jonathan Murray. I can give you his telephone number. He's my agent, an old friend. And a man called Brian Todd. I don't know how to contact him, but he's a partner in a firm of accountants in the city, so it wouldn't be hard to trace him."

"Anyone else?"

Curle hesitated. Haskell? Yes, Bobbie Haskell. But he lived in the same flats as Ali Fleming. And she was a secret, his secret life. He couldn't give Haskell's name. And then at once he realised that was no longer relevant. Meldrum had already asked him about her. Why?

And so at last he asked, "What is this about?"

80

CHAPTER
SIXTEEN

DI MELDRUM: I gather you were the one who reported that something was wrong, Mrs Johnson.

EVA JOHANSON: Johanson! My husband was Norwegian. He worked for a firm of shippers. Everyone in Edinburgh loved him, he threw such wonderful parties. It was only after he died — he dropped dead in the street, not a moment of warning, a heart attack, he was only fifty-one — it was only after that it was found he'd been using the firm's money for the parties. Not for himself, just transferring the money from elsewhere in his budget for the parties; you couldn't call it stealing. The firm honoured his pension.

DI MELDRUM: (slowly, impression of an unhurried patience) What made you worried enough about Miss Fleming to call the police?

EVA JOHANSON: Have you spoken to the young man upstairs? I don't know his name, isn't that silly? You'd think you'd know your neighbours, but you don't, not unless there's something wrong with the roof; it takes a crisis before you get to know people. You pass on the stairs and nod. Sometimes not even that. I don't remember even passing him all that often. I couldn't even tell you how long he's lived upstairs. People on my landing and the ones below me, you get their names from the doorplates. But he's on the top floor. You'll be able to find him.

DI MELDRUM: I'm sure we will. How does he come into this?

EVA JOHANSON: I heard him banging on Miss Fleming's door this morning! He told me he'd tried yesterday too. It seemed very strange that she wasn't answering.

DS McGUIGAN: How did you know she wasn't at work?

EVA JOHANSON: He'd phoned her work.

DS McGUIGAN: This man upstairs had phoned her work? Did he say why?

EVA JOHANSON: He was worried. I mean, I was worried too. Especially after I remembered the thumping noises.

DI MELDRUM: Thumping noises?

EVA JOHANSON: From upstairs! Last night.

DI MELDRUM: Noises from Miss Fleming's flat? Can you say more exactly what they were?

EVA JOHANSON: *Thumping* noises.

DI MELDRUM: Like someone walking heavily?

EVA JOHANSON: No! I know what that sounds like! When my husband and I lived in Brussels, the woman above us had parquet flooring. The noise was terrible. When I complained, she made even more of a racket. Stamp, stamp, stamp. I asked if she could wear slippers in the flat. Slippers are for peasants, she told me. High heels and painted an inch thick. I was sure she was the retired Madam of a brothel. Let it go, my husband said, laughing at me, you'll get us in trouble. God knows what kind of friends she has!

DI MELDRUM: Not someone walking around then . . . So what did it suggest to you?

EVA JOHANSON: (lowering her voice) A struggle. I thought it was a fight. Moving around. Falling down. Like I said, thumping noises.

DS McGUIGAN: You didn't go up to see what it was?

EVA JOHANSON: Because I went up this morning? Knocking isn't the same thing as thumping at all. Last night I was in my bed. It's easier to be brave in daylight.

DI MELDRUM: Can you place the time you heard these noises last night?

EVA JOHANSON: I was sleeping and I woke up. I do that. I read in bed and fall asleep. Sometimes I wake up in the morning and I still have my glasses on. The lamp was still on when I woke up, but I knew it was still night. Then I heard the noises and knew what had wakened me. After a while, they stopped. Someone's won, I thought. It took me a while to get back to sleep.

DI MELDRUM: Do you have a bedside clock? Did you check the time?

EVA JOHANSON: I don't think I did.

DI MELDRUM: So you couldn't place the time for me?

EVA JOHANSON: Oh, yes. It must have been not long before midnight. I got up to make a cup of tea because I was upset and when I was bringing it back the clock in the living room was chiming twelve. The noises must have been half an hour or twenty minutes before that.

DS McGUIGAN: (clears his throat)

EVA JOHANSON: (sharply) I'm sorry if I talk too much. I don't talk to many people now. It's funny all those people we knew. They seemed to disappear when the parties stopped.

BOBBIE HASKELL: I'm not usually home as early as that. I got away early from the shop because I was feeling unwell. (Laughs uneasily) I put it down to the winter bug. Truth is, I'd been out drinking with friends the night before. I'm not a big drinker and I must have had more than usual. I felt terrible the next day, and by the afternoon I'd had enough.

DI MELDRUM: About what time did you get back to the building?

BOBBIE HASKELL: Some time after five. As I came along the street, I saw this man at the door. When I saw it was Ali's buzzer he was pressing, I told him she would be at her work. That's when he told me who he was. Mr French, the man she worked for. I took him upstairs and he banged on her door. I mean, he knocked, but it was really loud knocking. When he went off, he gave me his card so that I could phone if she turned up. Sorry. (Wiping his eyes.) I still can't believe it.

DI MELDRUM: Take your time.

BOBBIE HASKELL: I tried that night more than once. I just couldn't think of any reason why she wouldn't be at home. No luck. Tried again this morning and that's when Mrs Johanson got involved. She was the one who called the police, do you know that? They were here when I got home from work. I can't tell you anything else.

DI MELDRUM: How well did you know Miss Fleming?

BOBBIE HASKELL: We were friends.

DI MELDRUM: Close friends?

BOBBIE HASKELL: What does that mean? Are you asking were we lovers?

DS McGUIGAN: Were you?

BOBBIE HASKELL: No! We were friends. That was enough.

DI MELDRUM: You would describe yourself as a close friend though?

BOBBIE HASKELL: I don't find it hard to make friends. I was only in my flat a few months when I got talking to Ali. She had an armful of books and was having difficulty getting her key into the lock. So many books, I thought she must be a great reader! She wasn't, in fact — not the way I am — they were for research, a project she was working on. She was an artist, you know. We liked one another at once.

DI MELDRUM: Firm friends then. Did you spend much time with her?

BOBBIE HASKELL: We talked every week. Sometimes just a word or two. Sometimes we'd have a coffee and a natter. We had a few meals together. Mostly in my flat; she didn't like to cook!

DS McGUIGAN: Did she ever confide in you?

BOBBIE HASKELL: About how she felt? Oh, yes! For example, when I met Mr French it was quite strange. She'd told me so much about him, what a slave driver he was. And here was this fat little man with just a few white hairs over his scalp banging on her door and looking so flustered.

DI MELDRUM: What about other friends?

BOBBIE HASKELL: . . . I don't know how many other friends she had. Sorry.

DS McGUIGAN: Was she in a relationship with anyone?

BOBBIE HASKELL: Yes.

DI MELDRUM: Did she tell you his name?

BOBBIE HASKELL: She didn't have to. She didn't ever talk about it, but I was sure there was someone. She was so discreet, I just knew it had to be a married man. And then when I met this man in her flat, I knew he had to be the one.

CHAPTER
SEVENTEEN

Curle started awake in the dark of the night and berated himself for a fool. What in God's name had he thought he was doing? He'd told them he didn't know Ali Fleming. He'd claimed to have gone straight home on the Tuesday night after leaving Jonah. They could probably prove that he knew her, probably prove that he hadn't gone straight home. If they could somehow also prove that he had seen her that night, then he would become the obvious suspect. His quick imagination in half a dozen images had him charged, in the dock, sitting in a prison van on his way to a life sentence. Beyond that, there were images he turned away from; he wasn't the kind of man who could cope with prison. How could he be anything else but a victim in that environment? If it comes to that, I'll kill myself, he thought. But even as he thought it, he disbelieved it; he wasn't the kind of man to commit suicide either. And with that he wondered about the book he might write when he got out of prison. Would you be allowed to write in prison? He didn't think he would have the strength of character for that. No Jeffrey Archer, he. And he saw himself at the other end of a prison sentence alone in a room, abandoned by everyone, too sunk in depression and self-contempt to do anything but stare at a wall.

Abandoned by Liz. He found that possibility unbearable.

Meldrum had asked her what time he had arrived home, and she had told him she had no idea since she had been feeling unwell and had taken a sleeping tablet and been asleep by ten o'clock that night. It was the truth, but what good was the truth? Anyway, Meldrum probably thought, a wife's testimony: she's lying to protect him. In that case, why not say he'd come home by eleven? Because she didn't know what it was all about. Because the detectives had taken him by surprise, given him no chance to tell her what to say. Or perhaps, Meldrum might think, because though she didn't want to condemn him yet she wouldn't lie for him; in which case claiming to have been asleep would be the easy way out.

He lay listening to her breath sighing, hesitating, starting again, and wondered if she was feigning sleep.

After the policemen had gone, he had lied to her, claiming he'd never heard of the dead woman. What else would he do, after eight years of lying to her about where he'd been and what he'd been doing?

He had shown nothing when the policeman told him Ali was dead. He was sure he had shown nothing. He was sure he had played the part of a man hearing of the death of a stranger.

What would that lack of emotion mean to them if they learned that he had been sleeping with her?

And he hadn't been hearing about the death of a stranger. He felt the warmth of the woman beside him and thought of that other warmth. Now cold. "Murdered," Meldrum had said. No details, they never gave details. But when he'd added, "No doubt about that," his face had seemed even grimmer than before. What had been done to her? His stomach heaved and as he slid, carefully, so carefully, out of the bed, his mouth filled with vomit.

He crossed the floor in the dark, closed the bedroom door softly behind him and made it into the bathroom. Leaning over the basin, he spat and heaved a little, threw cold water up into his face and scrubbed himself dry with a towel. He padded downstairs without putting on the light, guided by a hand trailing down the bannister. In the kitchen, the tiles struck up cold on his bare feet. He took the decanter of whisky from the cupboard, but when he took out the cork the sweet-flavoured smell made him sicken. Instead, he made a mug of instant coffee, took a few sips and emptied the rest into the sink. On impulse, he turned away from the foot of the stairs and went into the room he used as his study. The air felt cold and when he put down the switch the light fell with an effect of desolation on the desk with its blank computer and scatter of scribbled notes.

From the shelf of reference books, he took down *The Oxford History of the Classical World*. He had picked it as unlikely to be taken off the shelf by anyone else. Inside he'd concealed the notes he'd taken at times over the years, late at night, about what she had said or what they had done. Ruffling through the pages, he took out the first notes he came to, scribbled down on leaves torn from a notebook.

"I'll tell you a fantasy that works for me. I imagine I've married a man from some place far away. It's maybe a remote farm somewhere in Italy. We live with his mother and his brothers. His mother learns that he hasn't consummated the marriage and she decides to do something about it. She gets me up on the table on all fours and milks me with her witchy fingers. My husband stands watching helplessly with his big dark eyes. The mother says, 'My son's failure to breed the stupid city whore is about to be remedied.' And she goes round her sons and strokes their cocks with her scary witchy magic fingers.'

He sat at the desk looking at the page under the circle of the lamp. He had known the woman who thought up that stuff. What kind of woman could think of it? It wasn't something a man could make up, he thought. Had he really known her? And wondered at last: what kind of man had it been who came home and wrote these things down? Alone in the middle of the night, as he had been when they were first written, the notes began to seem like messages in a language of which he had lost the meaning and the years with Ali like a dream from which, however hard he struggled, there might be no way of wakening.

CHAPTER
EIGHTEEN

He opened his eyes reluctantly on another day. And then at evening morning is so far away. Some Irish writer said that. But wasn't it just as true, at morning evening is so far away? And then at morning evening is so far away. A Scottish writer said that. I said it, Curle thought. The bed was empty. He slid an arm out and the place beside him was cold.

When he made it downstairs, he put on the kettle and found an egg in the fridge. He was putting water in a pan when the kitchen door was pushed open. Water splashed on his arm.

"Christ, Liz! I nearly jumped out of my skin. What are you doing here?"

"I ran Kerr to school and came back."

"Are you not feeling well?"

"That's what I told Donald. I coughed down the phone."

"How will they manage without a pharmacist?"

"He'll get cover from one of the other shops."

She sat at the kitchen table and watched as he laid the egg into the pan. Defensively, he drew his dressing gown round him and fastened the belt. Using the palms of his hands, he smoothed down his hair. Without looking round, he asked, "Should you be in bed? I'll bring you up something."

"That's not what I came back for."

"I need to shave," he said, staring down at the water bubbling gently round the egg. With his fingertips, he rasped the stubble on his cheek. "Not like me to come down without shaving."

"We haven't been happy," she said, "but it never occurred to me you might have someone else. Not until last night. I feel stupid."

"You are being stupid," he said. "I told you last night. I don't know the woman. Never heard of her. The police came here because they found she'd made a note of my name and address. Among others, I suppose. They were just being thorough. Maybe she was a fan."

"Sit down and talk to me," his wife said.

He sat on the other side of the table.

"Maybe she was going to write a letter," he suggested. "Remember those crazy letters I got last year?"

"When they asked me to come back in, you were white as a ghost."

"No!" He was dismayed.

"Did you go white when they told you she was dead?"

"I don't like policemen. Tramping in here. Into my house. A lot of people feel that way."

"Don't insult me. Please." She had been watching his face; now she looked down at her hands folded on the table.

Moved by an old sympathy, perhaps by no more than a habit of his body, he put out his hand and covered hers.

She didn't pull them away, but went on, "I must have been very easy to deceive. You would hardly have to make any effort at all. As easy as that. I don't see how you wouldn't have come to despise me, even a little bit."

He knew he should break out in denials, but he couldn't, so great an effort, it was too much. And so, they sat in silence, until she got up and put off the gas where the egg was knocking in the pan.

CHAPTER
NINETEEN

Breakfastless, Curle was ready for lunch at the Arts Club. By custom, it was eaten communally at the large table set in the window. There were about a dozen of them that lunchtime, members and guests of members, those he had seen before and unknown faces in more or less equal numbers. The conversation, again by custom, was general around the table.

"I've biked since I was nine or ten," announced one of the strangers. "But this February, first of the month, I was out and didn't need gloves. That's never happened to me before. I've never not needed gloves on the first of February, not even in the south of England."

"More proof the climate's changing," said another. "Not that we need more; the evidence is overwhelming."

And a third: "I heard a scientist from London University on the radio. According to him, they haven't paid enough attention to sunspots. The mini ice age a couple of hundred years ago was caused by sunspots. They had braziers and dancing on the ice on the Thames."

"You can always buy a scientist," someone said. "Do you know that Exxon has set aside a budget of eighty billion dollars to argue against global warming? Or would it be millions, billions seems too much, doesn't it?"

"My daughter graduated from Bristol University last year. It was held in the Cathedral. There was an address by an ecologist. He told the graduands, you're the ones who have to change the world. My generation's failed, he told them. We can't go on with big cars and all the rest. We've got to change our ways."

"That would cheer them up."

"Youngsters get told that all the time. When I graduated just after the war, the Thirties generation told us the same thing. We failed, you change the world."

"Bristol Cathedral? Lovely setting for a graduation."

"Absolutely. The Provost welcomed us. Not a word about God. This is the way it used to be, he said, the Cathedral at the service of the community. We're very glad to see you here. First-class speech."

"Know what my son said to me? Turns out his partner doesn't want to have children. Dad, he said to me, would you mind not being a grandfather? I thought that was sweet."

And so on.

Curle contributed nothing, keeping his eyes on his plate as he steadily disposed of his stew. Beside him, Jonah Murray was also silent, though giving every appearance of following the conversation with keen interest.

Later, in the bar upstairs, settled in front of a bottle of Sangiovese, he gave a fat chuckle and said,

"Edinburgh, the city of conversation. Remind you of the great days of the Scottish Enlightenment?"

Curle lifted his head and asked, "Sorry?"

"You haven't been hearing a word, have you? What the hell's wrong?"

"I had —"

"I can't hear you." Jonah cupped a hand jocularly behind his ear.

"I had the police at my door last night."

His friend leaned forward in concern. "Not an accident in the car? For God's sake, don't tell me anyone was hurt."

"They came about this woman." He took a deep breath. "They came about this woman I knew."

"What woman?"

"I'm sorry to put this on you."

"Wait a bit . . . Is this the woman you've been having an affair with?"

Surprise jolted Curle out of his misery. He gaped and asked, "You knew?"

"Suspected."

"I have to tell someone. But I can't imagine how you knew."

"How did you imagine you could hide anything in Edinburgh? There's always somebody who spots something going on. And that somebody never fails to talk to somebody else. The whole town clatters with gossip. You know that."

"Haskell?" Curle asked, saying the first name that came into his head. And as Jonah looked blank, went on, "Bobbie Haskell. He was there when we'd a drink on Tuesday — after the National Library reading."

"The Velcro man? What has he got to do with it?"

"You don't know him?"

"First time I'd ever clapped eyes on him. Didn't have much to offer, I thought. Seems as if I was wrong."

"He lives in the same building as her."

"She has a name?"

"Ali Fleming."

Jonah looked intrigued. "Doesn't ring a bell. Not one of the names I've put under review the last couple of years. When do I get to meet her? Do I get to meet her?" He frowned. "Not sure that I should. Not sure that I want to. I have to say I'm very fond of that wife of yours."

"Don't worry about meeting her," Curle said. "She's dead."

Jonah looked more bewildered than shocked. "Some kind of car accident? Why would the police come to you?"

"She was found dead in her flat. Not an accident." And before Jonah could get it wrong again, he said almost with impatience. "She was murdered. It happened late on Tuesday evening apparently. But she wasn't found until yesterday."

"They don't suspect you?"

Curle rubbed a hand over his mouth. The thick aftertaste of stew on his palate made him nauseous. "They came to see me."

"Wait!" Jonah held up a finger to make his point more emphatically. "Tuesday evening! You were with me all the time. At the talk, then we went to the pub. We walked down to Princes Street. And I saw you into the taxi to go home. It's what they call an alibi. Call yourself a detective novelist? Nothing to worry about."

Curle took no more than a fraction of a second too long before he nodded, just enough to be too late.

"You did go home?" Jonah asked slowly.

CHAPTER
TWENTY

There was wine left in the bottle when Jonah got up to go, which was unheard of. To be fair, Curle reflected as he came out of Rutland Square to weave his way along the crowded pavement on the shop side of Princes Street, at least the agent hadn't pretended to have an urgent appointment. He'd got to his feet, leaned down and squeezed Curle by the shoulder. "I'll love you and leave you," he'd said, "I need some time by myself to think."

Curle knew he should go home. He had to honour the contract for the new book and already he was thousands of words behind schedule. He had an image of his study, a quiet room at the back of the house, looking out on to the garden. By contrast, his first book had been handwritten using a succession of cheap biros the summer before he went to university, crouched on a chair in his bedroom, trying to ignore the sounds of his father stumbling about downstairs. Not long after he was married, he'd begun yet another novel, hammering it out on a second-hand typewriter at a makeshift desk in the back room of their rented accommodation. Books that were left unfinished, ones that struggled to the last page, none of them published. Yet Liz had never stopped believing in him. Then Mae had been born and they had been happy. Five minutes earlier, five minutes later, and they might have gone on being happy. The timing had been precise and the lorry came out of the side street and smashed them across the road. He'd fought his way out of the car and into the back seat where he'd held Mae in his arms as her head fell to one side and the world went silent. The next year Liz went back out to work and his first novel was published and was enough of a success that he left the library and became a full-time writer. A book published at last and now he had a house with a study, the kind of room the boy had dreamed of having, the young man had dreamed of having. He had betrayed them both.

Afraid to go home, he wandered the length of Princes Street and then up the Bridges. He went into a bookshop and left in a panic for fear it was the one where Bobbie Haskell worked. He read the posters outside the Festival Theatre as if studying for an exam, and pacing on desultorily could not remember a word of what he had read. In Melville Drive the sun slanted between the trees and joggers ran with slack fists and swinging arms around the perimeter of the Meadows. By the time he got to Bruntsfield, he was tired and thought about going into the hotel for a coffee and then, for no better reason than that one was pulling up as he arrived at the stop, got on a bus that would take him home.

He sat on the front seat upstairs, watched the light changing on the Pentland Hills as they went up through Morningside and thought how it must be desirable in every city to be on the side that caught the morning sun. Leave the cold side to the poor, which must be why an East Ender from London or Glasgow was prone sooner or later to bore you with hints of hardness. Fuck off and learn to appreciate the sunset, he thought, and kept up the same distracting chatter in his head in place of thought even on the short walk after he'd left the bus until he was confronted by his own house, cosy as an egg in a nest of similar properties laid by a builder fifty years earlier.

As he pushed open the garden gate, the chatter in his head quietened leaving him with the single thought: I want to be forgiven. More than anything else he wanted to be forgiven.

He went round the side of the house and tried the kitchen door. It was unlocked. Liz must be at home. It was an old point of dispute that she never locked it. He was a compulsive locker of doors. He checked his watch; too early for Kerr to be home from school. He squinted into the empty kitchen and then closed the door softly and went on into the garden. At the corner, he stood motionless watching little birds acrobatically pecking at a container of nuts he'd hung from one of the naked branches of the cherry tree. Abruptly, he swung about, the birds flew off and he went at last into the house.

In the utility room, he kicked off his shoes and put on the slippers he kept in a box under the work surface. Going through into the hall, he hung his coat in the cupboard and had his hand out to open the front-room door when he heard the murmur of a man's voice.

Brian Todd, his Judas-coloured hair pale in a shaft of winter sun from the window behind him, put down his coffee cup as Curle went in.

"I'm so glad you're back before I had to go," he said. "Your wife was just getting ready to collect your son from school."

He was on the couch by the window, Liz in one of the easy chairs placed opposite the television.

"If I don't go now, I'll be late," she said getting up. She looked down at Todd and said carefully, "I'm sure you meant to be helpful."

Curle followed her into the hall. "What the hell is he doing here?" he whispered.

"The police have spoken to him too," she said in the same guardedly polite tone, like a woman concealing her symptoms from a doctor. Before he could respond, she was gone.

Curle took the seat she'd left. A dozen thoughts went through his mind. At last he said, "The school isn't far away. She'll be back in twenty minutes."

"Does she go for him every day?"

"There are two main roads."

"Oh, yes."

The questioning note was so faint that it might not have been there at all, yet Curle felt it as a criticism of his son. Yes, there are crossing patrols. Yes, other children come home by themselves. You didn't lose a child, you bastard.

Stupid to say any of that.

"I can't imagine how you found where I lived."

"Looked you up in the phone book," Todd said.

"We're not in the phone book."

Todd smiled, not at all put out. "You're a public figure," he said easily. "One of my partners does work for the Arts Council. You were in one or another list of writers."

"I still don't understand . . ."

"Why I'm here? Like your wife said, believe it or not, I wanted to see if there was any way I could help."

"I don't need help."

Todd put his head to the side and studied him thoughtfully.

After this became intolerable, Curle said, "My wife tells me the police have been to see you."

"Two of them. The one that mattered was called Meldrum. Big chap. Grim face. He looks as if life has disappointed him." He nodded as if pleased with himself. "I can see you recognise the description."

"What did he want?"

Todd made a face at the stupidity of the question. "They wanted to talk about that night in the pub after the National Library do."

"What has that got to do with me?"

"Oh, come off it. It was all about you. They were very particular about when you left. I'm afraid I was rather vague about exactly when that might have been. It's not the kind of thing you make a note of, not on an evening out."

"I still don't see why you've come here."

"You have a view of me from school. I think what happened then mattered more to you than to me. I honestly can't understand why you would still care

104

about it. You're very successful, a public figure like I said. I've read bits about you in the papers. Same thing with me, I'm a successful man. I'm not that boy." As he leaned forward his face seemed shiny with sincerity. "Believe me, I do want to help."

Curle felt as if he'd been put in the wrong in some way he couldn't quite understand. "Even so," he said, "I can't see how you could."

"For one thing, I know what happened that night. If that's any good to you."

Curle felt his heart begin to pound. He forced himself to keep still. As he waited for Todd to accuse him of being with her that night — how could he know? who else knew? how could he know? — he grew afraid that the beating of his heart could be heard.

"Thing is," Todd said, "they can't ask questions without giving something away. By the time they'd finished I was sure there had been a murder. It wasn't hard to check the papers and decide which one. The bit of luck was that I recognised the byline on the newspaper report as belonging to a client of mine who hadn't filled in a tax return for five years. He came to me after the Revenue caught up and I got him out of the mess. A phone call and he filled in the blanks — the bits that weren't in the papers." He paused. It was Curle's chance to say he didn't want to hear any more, but he couldn't bring himself to do that. Satisfied, Todd went on, "She was beaten on the face and body. On the body, she'd been kicked, front and back, breasts and stomach, kicked in the kidneys, stamped on. The worst, though, was her face. Most of the bones in it were broken. With those kinds of injuries, she could have choked on her own blood, had a brain haemorrhage. One of the kicks had ruptured her spleen, she could have died of that. Whoever the killer was, he didn't leave anything to chance. After the beating, she was choked so hard that her voice box was crushed."

"How could you imagine knowing any of that horror would help me?"

He felt an overwhelming desire to vomit. Bad food you could sick out of your system, bad thoughts once they were in there was no way to get rid of them. All the time Todd had been talking, he'd watched each word shaped from his mouth as though hypnotised. Without the intensity of that focus, he would have failed to catch a fleeting compression of the wide narrow lips. He was certain of the movement, but unsure at once of what it might mean, though at first he had thought it could only be the flickering suppression of a smile.

"Maybe I wasn't thinking straight," Todd said. "Knowing someone involved in a murder is a new experience for me."

CHAPTER
TWENTY-ONE

"He said you were at school together." She spoke quietly as they sat at the kitchen table, still cluttered with dishes from dinner. From the front room gunshots sounded faintly; Kerr was watching an old Western. "Was that true?"

"He made my life intolerable for a while."

"You never mentioned him to me."

As he looked at her and the silence went on, he had a sudden memory of the afternoon at school when Harriet Strang had slapped Todd's face. Stop it! she'd said, her voice trembling with nerves and rage. Leave him alone! He's had enough! Todd had stared at her in shock, but just then the teacher came back into the lab and the lesson went on. By the time it was over, Todd was his usual smiling self and nothing was changed. No, that wasn't true. Things were worse, a girl had defended him, of course it was worse. How could he ever tell Liz any of that?

"Telling everything? That's a lovers' illusion," he said, and hated her for a moment. "Most people grow out of it."

"Is that when they start to keep secrets?"

"Leave it!"

"Keep your voice down!" She glanced towards the distant sound of guns fired in anger. After a moment, she said, so softly he could hardly hear her, "Thing is, I don't have any secrets."

"It was over," he said. "I'd told her before . . . it happened."

"Before she was murdered."

"I'd told her it was over."

"You'd stopped seeing her?"

"I'd told her." It was too hard to explain.

"We weren't happy," she said, "but I never thought of another woman. It just didn't occur to me. You must think I'm an awful fool. Even after the policemen came, I believed what you told me. I suppose I did know really, but it was as if I couldn't focus, you know when you put those drops in that make your eyes blur? It was talking to your friend Todd that made me see."

"Is that what he came for?" Curle asked, questioning himself as much as her.

But she dismissed that. "He didn't tell me anything. It was just that what he said took it for granted she was your mistress. I'm sure he thought I must know."

"You know what he thought? I don't think so," Curle said. "God knows what goes on in his head."

"So why did he come? What did he say to you?"

"You want to know, I'll tell you. I don't want to have any secrets," he said, aware he was being a bastard. "He came to tell me how she was killed. I don't know how he knew. He claims some reporter told him. If you can believe him, she was kicked and stamped until she was broken inside. Whoever did it beat her face into a pulp. And after all that she was strangled."

She put up her hands as if pushing something away. It was a gesture he might have anticipated. How could his words not shock her? If there was shock in her look, however, there was something else as well.

"Did he really say that?" she asked, and he understood that the time was past when she would believe everything he told her.

"Yes."

"This is a bad dream."

"I'll tell you what's worse," he said. "I recognised the description."

As she stared at him blankly, he felt an irrational moment of anger.

Doesn't anyone read my books properly? he wondered.

In his last three books, Jack's Friend had beaten women to death and afterwards strangled them in some grotesque effort to seal their dying.

CHAPTER
TWENTY-TWO

The bench he'd chosen should have been a haven since it was set on the far side of a grass enclosure behind the towering hedge that sheltered the demonstration gardens. Just after he'd sat down, a young man in a green anorak took the bench in the other corner, put his radio down beside him and switched it on. He didn't put it on loudly, might even have thought he was playing it only for himself, which made the impact worse since all that carried was the pulse of some percussion instrument marking a triple rhythm endlessly, soft-loud-loud, like a head being bumped down a flight of stairs. The sky was overcast and the air was cold, but instead of moving off the man took out a packet from the side pocket of his anorak. Carefully unwrapped, it gave up what seemed to be a squashed sandwich, which he proceeded to eat as the tune changed and a new beat went on remorselessly.

As Curle picked over and over at the problem of why he hadn't been arrested, endless and unremitting came a spaced no-hurry thump-pause-thump like blows to the head of a helpless opponent.

He'd been collected from home the previous morning by Meldrum and DS McGuigan and taken to police headquarters. Alone in the house, he'd been too dispirited to resist their request or even to ask questions.

As he came out of the lift in the police building with a detective on either side of him, he saw Assistant Chief Constable Fairbairn approaching from the other end of the long freshly painted corridor. Even as he raised his hand in a kind of automatic greeting, he knew it was a stupid thing to do. All the same, he was shocked when Fairbairn spun on his heel and, without any pretence of dignity, hurried off the way he'd come. Involuntarily, he glanced up at Meldrum, who gave no sign of having noticed. They walked slowly in the opposite direction to a door at the end of the corridor. It led to a flight of stairs, which McGuigan with a touch on his elbow indicated they should descend. "Repairs on the side car park," he said. "Up and come down again's the fastest way at the moment."

As they came into a short corridor at the bottom of the stair, a door opened, giving a glimpse of a JCB digging up the car park, and a man came through. At sight of them, he stopped abruptly and turned back bumping into the uniformed officer who was following him. McGuigan sucked air through his teeth with a hiss. Curle had never seen the man before; he realised that he'd been expecting to see Bobbie Haskell. He glanced at Meldrum who was expressionless. As they walked on, he tried to reconstruct the face of the stranger. A man of about fifty with greying hair and patches of stubble in the corners of his jaw, wearing a padded jacket and jeans; he stirred not the faintest of recollections.

They came into the room at the end of the corridor to find a group of men already standing in line with the awkwardness of strangers at a bus stop. "Stand anywhere you want," McGuigan said. Curle couldn't decide whether the others in the line-up were policemen in plain clothes or members of the public. In either case, none of them bore much of a resemblance to himself. One had a white beard, another was well under average height. He counted eight places along and stepped into the line. Eight was his lucky number. Relieved, it even occurred to him that whoever the witness was there was a good chance he would identify somebody else.

Later, in the interview room, Meldrum said, "He's absolutely sure."

McGuigan added, "One hundred and ten per cent — his words."

"Sure of what?" Curle asked. He still felt detached from it all, waiting for them to admit their mistake.

"His name's Peter Stiller," McGuigan explained. "It took us some time to find him. But it was worth it. He's identified you as the passenger he took in his taxi to Ali Fleming's address in Royal Circus on the Tuesday night she died."

How can that be? he thought quite calmly. When I've never seen him before in my life.

"I can't imagine," he said aloud, "how a taxi driver would remember any passenger in particular. They must have so many."

He caught the glance that went between them, and understood that his first response should have been that he hadn't been anywhere near Ali's house that night.

"He picked you up in Princes Street and you gave him an address he doesn't remember," McGuigan said with an effect of being scrupulously fair. "As he recalls, though, it might have been your home address. Certainly in that direction. Halfway up Lothian Road, though, you changed your mind and gave him the Royal Circus address."

He paused as if for comment. Curle said sceptically, "You're saying he remembered this passenger because of a change of destination?"

"When the taxi arrived at Royal Circus, you asked him to wait for you," McGuigan went on. "But he had another call and refused. You lost your temper and called him a bastard. That made him angry, but he just took your money and drove off. He said he'd really wanted to punch you, but told us all the sensible reasons for not getting out of the cab. Apart from common sense, he gave the impression you'd frightened him. According to him, when you lost your temper it was very violent and sudden. I'd guess he was a bit ashamed of being frightened."

At last, Meldrum broke his silence. "That's why he remembers you," he said.

With that, Curle's resistance was over. He was one of those people for whom telling lies made for a sense of strain, which was why during the eight years of his affair he had never been perfectly at peace. True to type, once he'd started he gave up every detail. He told how he had met Ali Fleming, how they had become lovers, how hard he had tried to keep it a secret. His account of the last time he saw her was as accurate and full as recollection could manage. Too intelligent not to see that his account of breaking off with her could easily have had a different ending, one in which a threat from her to go to Liz might plausibly have ended in violence, yet he had no way of preventing himself from plodding stubbornly forward.

At the end, in a last spasm of honesty, he'd confessed, "I've no memory of the taxi driver. All I can say is that I don't usually swear at people."

McGuigan asked sympathetically, "Do you often lose your temper and then forget what happened?"

Ignoring that, Curle asked, "That was the taxi driver we met coming in from the car park, wasn't it?" And when neither of them answered, he realised belatedly, "Doesn't that mean his identification of me is useless?"

"Could be," McGuigan said, "but doesn't really matter now, does it?"

At some point not long afterwards, a swab was rubbed down the inside of his cheek. A sample of his DNA, they said, and he wondered what they held to match it against.

It had come as a surprise when he found himself in a police car again and not a cell. They took him home and he was grateful that it was still too early for Liz or Kerr to be there for it felt as if he had been away a very long time. The two policemen were gone by the time Kerr came home with one of the neighbours and her son who was a classmate. At half six, Liz came home and they ate and later that night he explained to her that the police had taken away some of his clothes and two pairs of heavy outdoor shoes and all the gloves that were his. But he didn't tell her how he'd asked, "Was he wearing gloves when he beat her?" and how at the question McGuigan had swung round from his task of clearing the drawer to stare at him.

Going over it again and again until the steady beat of music from the opposite bench throbbed in his head like a vessel ready to burst, he could find no explanation. Fairbairn had thought he was about to be arrested. McGuigan, he felt sure, must have wanted to arrest him.

Why had Meldrum not arrested him?

CHAPTER
TWENTY-THREE

Bobbie Haskell squealed as the door of Ali Fleming's flat opened.

"What? What's wrong?" The woman stared, one hand thrown up in alarm.

"Who are you?" Haskell came cautiously closer and, as if anticipating the same question explained, "I live in the flat upstairs."

"Are you Bobbie Haskell?"

Looking even more alarmed, Haskell nodded.

"My sister told me about you."

"I don't understand."

"I'm Ali Fleming's sister."

"Oh, dear." Trying to recover himself, he said, "When the door opened, I thought — I thought it was her."

"But I look nothing like her."

"It was just — I thought the flat was empty — seeing the woman shape. My heart's still pounding."

When the woman smiled, he saw that there was a resemblance, though Ali had been slimmer and taller and this woman had the solid build of a swimmer. She was probably in her late forties, so she might be ten years or so older than her dead sister, though he wasn't a good judge of age.

"I'd better warn you then, I'll be here for a bit."

"Is the flat yours now? I mean did Ali leave it to you?"

"It wasn't hers to leave," the woman said. She glanced behind her. "Do you want to come in? I was just going out to get some food, but there's milk for a cup of tea."

He failed to stop a shudder. "I couldn't. Not where it happened. How can you?"

"I'm managing."

Quick to meet a mood, he said, "I'm sorry! Look, why not come up to my place? We could have tea there. And a biscuit if you want."

As they climbed the stairs, the woman said, "I've made up the couch in the living room. I couldn't sleep in the bedroom."

Neuf points for sensitivity, he thought, but said aloud, "I'm so sorry about Ali. I was devastated. I should have said that at once, but I was so taken aback."

"My fault for giving you a fright. My name's Linda. Linda Fleming."

As he unlocked the door and led the way in, he said, "It's the same set-up as — as the flat below. That's the lounge through there. Have a seat and I'll bring tea."

Five minutes later, when he brought through the tray she was seated in the easy chair that had its back to the window. As he lifted a little table to the side of her chair, she crossed her legs and he was conscious of a faint smell of her sweat.

"They're such nice rooms," she said. "High ceilings. Did you furnish it yourself?"

"Every stick," he said. "The colour scheme's mine too. I bought the flat when I inherited money from an aunt. A wonderful buy, as things turned out."

"Downstairs belongs to my parents, always has done. My youngest sister lived in it after I had it for a while. Then Ali got the use of it. My parents are quite old and retired and I live in London."

He poured tea and offered her a choice of sweet biscuits laid out in a fan on an oval china plate with a blue border.

"I suppose it will be sold now," he suggested.

"Oh, yes."

She sipped her tea in silence while he tried to think of something else to say.

"We got on very well together," he said at last. "I'd like to think she thought of me as a friend."

"I wonder how many friends she had."

He shrugged and shook his head.

"There was a difference in your ages, of course," she said thoughtfully.

"Maybe she didn't have many friends!"

She looked at him. "That sounded almost spiteful."

"I didn't mean it that way," he said.

"Maybe she didn't have friends," Linda Fleming observed. "How would I know? There's no harm in saying something if it's true."

"Don't you know? I mean with you being her sister."

118

"Her sister in London. We weren't all that close."

"She did mention me, though, you said that." He leaned forward and frowned.

"Something had broken and you fixed it. She was very impressed."

He sat back smiling. "That happened more than once. I've always been good with computers and stuff. She wasn't very technically minded."

Linda Fleming nodded and seemed about to smile in response but then her eyes filled with tears.

"It hits you in unexpected ways," he said. "When my grandmother died, I was fine. I blamed myself for not feeling more. But when they were putting her coffin into the hole, the earth on the sides was damp and shiny. That upset me."

The woman looked down as if studying her hands folded in her lap. Without looking up, she said quietly, "I just wish we'd kept more in touch."

"Well," Haskell said, "I don't know if I should tell you, but there was somebody who seems to have been close to her."

"A friend?"

"A good deal more than that, I'm afraid. A man called Barclay Curle. He's a writer. Quite well known, but I wouldn't rate him all that highly, to be honest with you."

CHAPTER
TWENTY-FOUR

Meldrum frowned. "I'm not sure why you brought this to us. Why do you want me to look at it?"

"I think it will be obvious once you've read it," Curle said. "It's just a few pages. It wouldn't take long for both of you to look at it. It's a note I made of something Ali told me."

As Meldrum bent his head, Curle could envisage the words on each leaf he had torn from his notebook.

"I was late and he'd changed house. [This was the Classics Professor you told me about? — Yes, she said] It was pretty tense when I got there. There was a ritual of transformation we did — it sounds silly but it made a difference. I had to bath and then he'd inspect me. I wasn't allowed to be the least wet. This time he laid me down on the bed and put the blindfold on. Then he asked me how much I'd been online, who I'd met, what I'd done, how often I'd cum without thinking of him. It was all quite gentle but it made me very uncomfortable. Eventually he came up with a figure — forty-eight strokes I owed him for tardiness and general slutty inconsideration. Normally I could cope, but I heard the belt slide out from his trousers. He gave me six hard strokes — it was bearable, just bearable, but I had to count and he talked to me all the time, which made it hard to keep count. [Did he fuck you?] Then he fucked me, lying face down still; he took me from behind. [In the arse?] After another two sets of six he told me he was going to fuck me in the arse. I've only had two cocks in my arse and both times it was very painful and unpleasant. He's not very big but it must have excited him what he was going to do to me so that he was very hard. It hurt a lot. By the end of the afternoon, I was only up to twenty-four. It's going to be hard on you, twenty-four to be taken quickly, he told me. I didn't think I could do it. My arse was so sore as if it had been sandpapered. I'll tell you what he said. Six of the cane and we'll write off the rest of the strokes. He'd never caned me. He'd used his hand — and he could cause pain with that — and a belt and the flogger and the crop. [Was there a ritual?] He told me I had to kiss the cane before and after. And I had to count them. When the first blow came it was like a white light in my head."

With a grunt, Meldrum handed the sheets to McGuigan.

Turning to Curle, he said, "You told us you didn't have a key to Miss Fleming's flat. You refused it, wasn't that what you said? In case your wife found it."

"Yes."

"But you made this note and kept it? When did you do that?"

"I can't give you an exact date. Three years ago, maybe four. I did it from memory after I got home the same night she told me about what he'd done to her."

"What about your wife? Wasn't it a risk putting stuff like that on paper? Weren't you afraid of her finding it?"

"I'm a writer. I wanted to write down what she'd told me while it was fresh in my mind. If my wife had come across it, I'd have told her I was making notes for a novel. I make notes all the time."

"Notes like that?"

"Not exactly like that."

"Out of your imagination?"

"Yes. Or things I hear or see. Anything that might be useful."

Meldrum accepted the sheets back from McGuigan, and laid them on the desk. "Was this out of your imagination?"

Curle stared in surprise. "No!" he said indignantly. "It's what she told me. Word for word. I have an excellent memory."

"Those bits in the square brackets," McGuigan asked. "That's you talking to her?"

"Yes."

Meldrum took up the questioning from a different angle. "If you weren't worried about your wife finding these notes, why hide them inside a book in your workroom? Isn't that where you said you kept them?"

"I didn't have the nerve to leave them in the open. It's what I should have done. We don't always — what we do doesn't always make sense. It's an idea I've used in some of my books. We don't always behave logically. In everyday life, I mean. You must know that."

"We know you write fiction. Let me ask you again, why did you want us to look at this stuff?"

"Isn't it obvious? She had this perverse relation with a man who had a taste for cruelty. I should think you'd want to question him. Ask him where he was when she was murdered."

"You're suggesting he murdered her?"

"I'm only saying it's possible. When I came across this note I'd made, I thought it was my duty to let you see it."

"So that we would know there was another suspect?" McGuigan asked.

Curle stared at him in silence.

"You think we should interview him?" McGuigan asked.

"You'd want to, I should think."

"What's his name?"

"I don't know. She never said. But a Professor of Classics! How many of those are there?"

"I've no idea," McGuigan said. "Have you made enquiries yourself?"

Curle shook his head.

After a pause, Meldrum said, "If your wife had found this note, you were going to tell her it was for a novel, right? Isn't that in fact what it was? Something you made up?"

"Maybe for a novel," McGuigan said, "maybe not."

"No! Why would I have brought it here, if I'd made it up?" But, of course, McGuigan had already suggested an answer: to provide them with a suspect other than himself.

And now it was McGuigan who asked, "Did you find it sexually exciting writing this kind of thing?"

"Did you find it sexually exciting to read? . . . Sorry. Forget I said that. But whether it's sexually exciting or not isn't the point. What matters is whether she told me these things. And she did."

"There's another possibility," Meldrum said. "Suppose these are the notes of a conversation you had with Miss Fleming. In that case, the things you said to her, those bits you've put in the square brackets, we'd call those leading questions."

"I don't know what you mean."

"You say things and she comes up with something in reply. The way it reads to me, whether you realise it or not, you're suggesting things for her to say."

"I was involved, I wanted to hear what she'd say next," Curle said. "All right, I'll admit it, I was sexually excited. Of course I was. What's wrong with that?"

"Has it never occurred to you she might have been making it up?"

"Why would she do that?"

"Maybe she was trying to keep you interested?" Meldrum said. "In case you got tired of her."

Curle opened his mouth as if to reply, and found he could think of nothing to say.

CHAPTER
TWENTY-FIVE

Though it was hardly possible to imagine that Calvinist Meldrum getting sexually excited by reading the note of what Ali Fleming had said, the handsome McGuigan was a different proposition. The thought there might be a stiffness down there hidden by the desk had helped him to meet the detective's gaze as it was raised from the papers, and while he was being questioned lingered at the back of his mind like a shield or talisman until the formulation "leading the witness" came on him like a hammer blow. Useless to claim I don't understand; he had understood only too well. Why would she make it up? Just because she wanted to hold his attention? Could it possibly be true that she had loved him? For most of their affair, he had wanted to break it off and despised himself for not having the strength. Whatever it had been about for him, it had had nothing to do with love. Had he ever seen her clearly, made the effort to think of how things were for her? He had always been too self-absorbed. Something corrupt in her had fascinated him. For the first time, it occurred to him that he might be the corrupter. To go through the world without causing harm, how carefully a man would have to make his way. If things had been different, if she had killed herself for love, however impossible the idea still was for him, sitting at his desk that morning it seemed to him that he would never have got over the guilt.

The rest of the morning after the debacle he sat in front of the computer. At intervals he played solitaire and got it out at intervals, ace to king in four piles, far more often than when he'd played with cards. It must be rigged, he decided, to keep you interested. He decided this regularly but it didn't stop him playing, since he hated battleships and had to play something. Some writers read the Bible before they started work, some sharpened pencils, he played solitaire. About noon when he'd added three sentences to Chapter 3 of the novel, the doorbell rang.

The sky behind the woman was the darkest shade of grey as if it might be about to yield up snow.

"Mr Curle? I think you knew my sister."

"I don't think so," he said firmly, but laughing at the same time since he had no objections to being interrupted by a reasonably good-looking woman. "Who might that be?"

"Ali Fleming."

Shocked, he blurted, "How did you know where to come?"

"Your friend Brian Todd gave me your address. Can I come in?"

He actually found himself looking beyond her. There were no witnesses in the empty street. It would be hours yet before Kerr came home. He stood aside and she came past him into the hall.

Seated in the front room, he asked, "How on earth do you know Brian Todd?"

"I don't know him. Bobbie Haskell gave me his number."

It was possible. That night in the pub, Jonah and he had left Haskell and Todd still drinking together.

As if to forestall any more questions, she said, "I'm staying in Ali's flat until the funeral."

"The funeral . . ."

"She's to be buried in Glasgow beside her grandmother. It's what Ali would have wanted. She cared for her grandmother more than anyone in the world."

He had never heard of this grandmother. I didn't know Ali at all, he thought. She could have told me. I would have listened.

"I'm very sorry." He never knew what to say to the bereaved. Shuffling out with the other mourners, shaking hands with relatives lined up at the church door, that's when it would be useful to be a Christian, "I'll pray for you", or an Irish peasant, "God be with you in your sorrow", little ritual containers that would hold as much feeling as you had to pour into them; as a Protestant atheist he was prone to mumbling.

She looked at him in silence. In her early forties at a guess, he couldn't see any resemblance to her sister. She had strong features, handsome rather than pretty. Despite himself, he couldn't help noticing the swell of her thighs under her skirt and the long smooth muscles of her calves.

"I was waiting for you to say that," she said. "I was beginning to think you'd never get round to it."

127

"You know about us."

"That's why I'm here."

"I had nothing to do with her death." Tears prickled in his eyes, taking him by surprise. He was ashamed of them in front of her sister, afraid that she would think he was play-acting. "And I am sorry."

It seemed after that the atmosphere changed. However strange it was, he felt as if for the first time he was able to share with someone his aching sense of the tragedy of Ali's death. At one point, he asked again about the funeral and was told that the police would release the body the following day and that the funeral would take place the day after.

"I'd like to be there," he said. "The family wouldn't need to know. I'd stay well back."

Later again, she suddenly said, "By the way, I should have said. I'm Linda."

"Ali told me she had two sisters," he said. "I don't remember her telling me your name."

"Did she say Rosalind?" And went on before he could shake his head, "From Shakespeare. It was hell at school when we did *As You Like It*. My youngest sister avoided that. My father called her Jean. He'd lost interest in strange names by the time she came along."

"Alexina," Curle said. "The police told me."

"Did they? No, Alexia. My father got it into his head that it was a beautiful name. She looked it up when she was fifteen and found it wasn't a Christian name at all — it's a medical condition. It means word blindness. That's when she became Ali."

128

He began to laugh, then stopped because it seemed inappropriate. The laugh had been genuine, however. "I'm grateful to you for talking to me like this. I don't know why . . ." He trailed off. Had he really been about to say something like, I don't know why you should trust me? That would have been stupid.

"Why? Because Ali phoned me every week. I feel as I've known you for the last eight years."

"She talked about me?"

The thought dismayed him. He imagined a portrait to make her sister despise him.

"You know how much she loved you?" Linda Fleming asked. "I don't think she ever gave up hope that you would leave your wife and be with her."

Bewildered, he blurted out the simple truth. "I couldn't ever have done that. I have a son."

"Parents leave their children all the time now."

"Not me."

"I'm glad you never spelled that out. She told me, if you left her she would kill herself."

He shook his head in denial. He couldn't believe that. It wasn't possible that she could have felt so strongly. How had love come into what was between them?

". . . I had no idea."

"Poor Ali," her sister said.

". . . You couldn't have been mistaken?"

"Poor Ali," she said again and this time, whether it was truly there or not, he seemed to hear a shade of contempt.

They sat in silence for so long that he thought that was the end of it.

When she began to speak again, her tone was more withdrawn, her voice softer as if sharing a confidence. "She spoke of this man Haskell too. I can't remember the first time she mentioned him. I've been trying to remember if she told me how they got talking. I have the impression she'd known him for some time before she first mentioned him to me. He fixed things for her, electrical stuff. She wanted to move a sideboard from the front room into her bedroom, but it was too awkward for her to manage on her own. He helped her. Ali was always like that. She'd always find someone to help her. She took him pretty lightly, almost as a joke, I don't mean in a nasty way. The faithful swine, she called him. The faithful swine was down last night, asking if there was anything I needed, I'd a job getting rid of him. That's how she'd talk. That stopped though. She didn't mention him much at all. But then apparently one night he was there when you turned up."

Curle waited but she seemed lost in thought. "Like you said, he was mending something."

"She didn't ask him to do that. He'd come down without being asked to see if she needed anything. He'd started doing that. She said he gave her the creeps."

He stared at her. "I'm not sure what you're saying."

"Do you think I'm sure?" She shook her head. "I haven't told him Ali and I spoke every week. I've given him the impression we were out of touch, that I knew nothing of her life. I even let him tell me about you.

When I speak to him, I have to be careful not to mention the things she's told me." She looked up and held his gaze. "I try to be careful."

"Have you told the police?"

"It's nothing they'd pay attention to. And if they did and questioned him, he'd know it came from me. All I can do is talk to him. Maybe he'll give something away. And maybe I'm grasping at straws and it's all nonsense. All the same . . . I'm being careful."

CHAPTER
TWENTY-SIX

Curle had parked his car a street away and waited until the last moment before going into the church. His idea had been to sit unnoticed at the back and slip out again just before the service ended. To his dismay there was no back any more. The church had been converted so that the pulpit had been removed from the chancel and now stood against the east wall of the nave with the congregation arranged on padded blue benches set in a half circle around it. As he slipped into the last row, curves of empty seats separated him from the group of no more than a dozen people who seemed huddled together for comfort in front of the empty pulpit. He assumed they were Ali's family, but when a figure much taller than the others turned to look at him he saw that it was the policeman Meldrum. It hadn't occurred to him that a policeman would come to her funeral. He bent his head over a hymn book and read the same verse over and over until after what seemed an interminable wait the service began.

There were stained-glass windows at either end of the nave, but the pulpit had been situated under tall windows of plain glass so that the congregation was in the full light of a low morning sun and the minister in

132

shadow. As uncomfortable as a tyro extra on a stage, Curle sat staring at his knees or squinting against the sunshine. He imagined the minister in his shadowy pulpit staring down and wondering who the solitary man, an isolated figure in all that brightness, might be. When it was over, he could not have repeated anything which had been sung or said, but was left with the sense that the minister, embellishing scraps given by her family, mouthing the platitudes of hope to set against the facts of mortality, had never met Ali Fleming, not even once in all her life.

He hurried out before anyone else and made the safety of his car intending to set out at once for home. As he pulled out, however, the hearse like a black fish nosed across the end of the street, and he turned after it, following the three or four cars that made up the procession. He could see that Meldrum drove the one immediately in front of him, and he was sure the policeman must know he was following. They moved slowly past a stretch of waste ground and then more quickly along an avenue of bungalows until they came into streets of brown tenements. Once he was held up at traffic lights and thought he had lost them, but caught up again as the hearse led them past a supermarket and not long afterwards through the cemetery gates.

It was an old urban settlement of the dead and the cars made their way after the hearse along one narrow path after another winding up between untended graves, overgrown with tangles of briar, grass and weeds. Curle who had been lagging had to brake as a

Land Services vehicle pulled out in front of him. It turned right into a path narrower than any so far and he inched along until it came to a stop blocking further progress.

Getting out, he walked slowly up to where the minister had already started the burial service. Perhaps, Curle thought, he couldn't wait because he too found the desolation of the place intolerable. A green tarpaulin was spread over the earth piled beside the open grave. Behind the cemetery wall, a shoddy grey high-rise pockmarked with tiny windows rose up like a cliff face of ugliness.

As Curle stood a little way off watching the mourners, he was moved to pity for Ali Fleming. Even the name they would carve on the tombstone under her grandmother's would be that exotic name she had rejected. Thinking of it made her seem a stranger again. "Can you read without moving your lips?" he had asked the first time they met. Absurd, drunken, inanely aggressive question; but then all of it was absurd, their meetings, the long interlocking of their imaginations, their fantasies. How much of her life had that time given to him been? How much had it mattered to her? He thought of almost the last time they'd been together and of a dream she had told him — she had been in a shop, a very small space; this man had tried to come in, he had a pack on his back, no room, as she tried to squeeze past him and get out his bulk pressed her back over the counter. It had been so unlike her usual fantasies that he had been disappointed, and so now he thought that perhaps it had been a true dream. He was pierced by the mystery of her and that she was dead and he would never have the chance to ask her all the questions that came to him now and none of them to do with sex. What did it matter what name she was given on the stone? Who would come to this forgotten corner to see it? In time, it would wear away as the names were wearing from all the stones around them. The group by the grave stepped back as the minister stopped speaking and Meldrum, bending down, was speaking to the sister. As they turned and looked at him, he felt the wetness of tears on his cheeks and realised that he had been crying. What were they thinking as they looked at him? Wasn't there an old saying that the criminal couldn't resist making an appearance, scene of the crime, scene of the grave.

He turned and forced himself to walk slowly back down to his car, expecting to hear a voice behind him. The Land Services vehicle was empty and still blocking his way. He stood beside it watching as the cortege disappeared. After a time the two workmen, who had no room to pull the vehicle aside for him and presumably didn't want to go ahead, came back and told him, "You'd be as well to back up. It's all brambles ahead and you'll get your car scratched."

Slowly Curle reversed down the path until he could turn and make his escape.

CHAPTER
TWENTY-SEVEN

"Do you like it?" Jonah Murray asked, waving a proprietary hand as Curle sat down. "Don't you think it lives up to its billing?"

"This place?" Curle looked around. "What about it?"

"You don't see a change? From the last time you were here?"

Curle thought about it. He'd last been in Jonah's office at the top of a winding stone staircase in the Pleasance during the Edinburgh Festival the preceding August when the agent had held a party for his clients and visiting celebrities.

"All I remember about that is getting drunk and spilling a glass of wine over that woman from A and P Watt."

"Your most embarrassing moment."

"No," Curle said. "My most embarrassing moment was being introduced to Muriel Spark. Mind a blank, I told her how much I'd enjoyed *Do Not Disturb*. It was like watching an apple shrivel in a snowstorm. After a while, she parted her lips and whispered *Not to Disturb*. And that was that." Jonah laughed. "It was a quote from Shakespeare apparently. I should have stuck to *The Prime of Miss Jean Brodie*. Never read it, but I could have told her I enjoyed the film."

"Novelists like to be told that." Jonah waved a hand again. "Don't change the subject. What do you think of it?"

"You've had it done up?"

"God, you are so unobservant. Remind me, what do you do for a living?"

"I'm a student of human nature not a pansy decorator."

"This month's *Scottish Homes and Interiors* has a lyrical piece about how I transformed a neglected flat into a masterpiece of modern taste." He spoke with the satisfaction of a self-publicist who made more of an impact on the media than most of his clients. "They don't usually do offices."

"Well," Curle decided after a thoughtful look around, "it isn't quite one any more, is it? Take the computer and stuff from through there where Alice does her secretarial stuff and you'd have a bedroom. Easy enough after what you've done here to imagine it as a sitting room. And you've done up the kitchen. Office back into flat, it'll sell for a nice profit when you're ready to bugger off back to London."

"Cynicism isn't an attractive trait." He glanced at his watch. "So what can I do for you?"

Curle took a breath and tried to keep the tension out of his voice. "Last time I saw you, you were going off for a think. So what have you thought?"

"This isn't the best place to talk about . . . what's happened. And I've someone coming in to see me."

Curle jumped to his feet. "Fine. My apologies."

Two strides took him to the door. As he opened it, he got a glimpse of Alice at the computer turning to look over her shoulder.

Behind him, he heard Jonah crying, "Oh, for God's sake!" as he bustled up out of his chair. Then the door was taken out of his grasp and closed. The agent stood close, glaring at him. "The moment of truth! You want the moment of truth? I was absolutely taken aback when you told me you were at that woman's flat the night she was killed."

"Not 'that woman'. She had a name. Her name was Ali Fleming."

"Well, bloody exactly. That matters to you. And I don't, not for one second, believe that you killed her. That's my thought, if it matters to you. I know all the stuff about everyone's capable of murder. Don't imagine I didn't think about that. And about all the pervasive stuff we live with that tells us every man's an island, we're all separate from one another, you can't ever see what's going on in someone else's mind. Fuck all of that. I've known you for a long time. All right, you had an affair. But if you killed that woman, above all if you killed her in that hellish way, then every face I've ever met is nothing but a mask. I don't want to live in a world like that."

He reached out and squeezed Curle's shoulder. Apart from handshakes, it was their first physical contact since schooldays.

Curle went back and sat down again. He had come for a verdict without any belief it would be in his favour since, for ever it seemed, he had been an advocate of the idea that no one could be sure of what went on behind another man's eyes: a notion he'd drawn on glibly enough in his novels. He felt, at least for the moment, absolved. He was moved by the other man's trust and made ashamed by it. He rested his face between his hands and said quietly, "I'm pretty frightened."

Jonah settled one buttock on the edge of his desk and swung his leg in tiny arcs back and forward. "They'll get whoever did it."

"I don't know why they haven't arrested me already."

"That must mean something. Maybe they have a suspect we don't know about."

"Ali's older sister came to see me. She's living in the flat."

"Where her sister was killed? How morbid of her!"

Curle hesitated. "Do you remember Bobbie Haskell?"

"Who?"

"The young guy who fastened on to us after the talk at the Library. Said he worked in a bookshop."

"And came to the pub? The Velcro man? What about him?"

"Linda Fleming thinks he's the killer."

Jonah's leg stopped at the top of its arc and sank.

"How extraordinary!"

"I don't believe it either. She said Ali told her he'd been making a nuisance of himself. I can't see him as a murderer, though, can you?"

Jonah shook his head. "Nuisance, certainly. Not a murderer."

"Anyway, she turned up at the house. Luckily Liz was at work. She claimed Brian Todd gave her my address." He glanced up with a glint of suspicion. "I wonder how he got it in the first place."

"Ask him."

"I suppose I could."

"No. I mean now. He's due any minute."

"Here?"

"Just business. He's coming in to discuss a book." At Curle's blank stare, he smiled. "Everyone has a book in them. Only one, in most cases. Half my success has been in sniffing out the right one."

"But why him?"

"He approached me. He's anxious it seems to dig some dirt."

"On his clients? Why on earth would he want to do that?"

Before Jonah could answer, his assistant Alice tapped and put her head round the door.

"Mr Todd's here."

CHAPTER
TWENTY-EIGHT

It didn't matter where he tugged, every end was a loose one. He'd walked out as Brian Todd walked in, feeling as Jonah had said earlier that the agent's office was no place for asking questions about Ali Fleming's death. Chances were, he decided, that it had anyway been Jonah who had given his address to Todd. He couldn't imagine why Todd would have asked for it, but he knew Jonah too well to have any difficulty with the idea of him giving it cheerfully and without a second thought. It was even possible that Jonah, that lover of gossip, might at this moment be sharing with Todd the risible image of Bobbie Haskell as Ali's killer.

He chewed over that unsavoury morsel all the way home on the bus, staring out of the window determinedly when the man seated next to him showed signs of wanting to start a conversation. With parking scarce in Edinburgh and a bus service that was fast and frequent, it made sense to take the bus into the centre. Sometimes that meant talking to people. Occasionally, he'd even found it useful. He'd a bad habit of incorporating snatches of conversation into his novels, a kind of found art like pieces of driftwood sculpted by the tides. On the other hand, sometimes it wasn't all right and he'd find himself wishing that more Edinburgh people would live up to their reputation for reserve. On bad days, he tended to put the phenomenon of being accosted down to the number of unfortunates released into the care of the community.

He escaped from the bus a mile or so before his usual stop and walked home. It was lunchtime but, too restless to stay in the house, he took the car from the garage with some vague idea of running into the country. On impulse, however, after he'd crossed the main road he turned into the street that led to Kerr's school and pulled up a few hundred yards beyond the entrance. As he walked back, he could hear the babble of children before he came in sight of them. Watching as they scurried around in a frenzy of Brownian motion, there was no way of telling if they were agitated by enjoyment or anxiety in these last moments of freedom before the bell summoned them inside. Almost when it was too late, he spotted his son standing by himself in a corner of the playground. Shoulders hunched, he seemed to be studying the ground at his feet, his stillness among all that activity infinitely pathetic. For the first time, it occurred to Curle that his son might be a victim of bullying. With a convulsive gesture he threw his hand into the air and, as Kerr lifted his head, waved him to approach.

"We're going for a run. Come on."

Kerr had to hurry to keep up.

"Should we tell the teacher?"

"Don't worry about it. I'll give you a letter to her."

In the car, the boy asked, "What will Mummy say?"

"Don't look so worried." Please don't look so worried. "I won't tell her if you don't. All right?"

". . . Where are we going?"

"Where would you want to go?"

"Some of the boys in the class have seen *The Invincibles*. Is it on anywhere?"

"The sun's shining." He wanted to talk to his son. Not sit beside him in the dark letting the time pass when too much of it had passed already. "We could go to the zoo."

"Won't it be closed?"

"It's open all the year round. It's interesting at this time of the year."

As he drove down Lothian Road, however, intending to take the Western Approach out to Corstorphine, he recalled how on free afternoons in the first job he had after leaving school in Glasgow he would go to the zoo. He had a memory of mangy beasts in cramped cages and a sudden image of a lone polar bear in a narrow pit rocking endlessly back and forward. The Edinburgh zoo was different, he told himself: wide open paddocks climbing the sides of a lofty hill. When they got there, though, it was snowing. He sat in the car park looking at the fat flakes spinning down. What a bloody country! How could sun and blue skies transform so fast into grey clouds and snow?

"Let's sit for a minute. It might clear up again."

In a moment the snow condensed into little stones, little white stones of hail that drummed a deafening tattoo on the roof and clogged the windscreen.

"What a country!"

"I don't have gloves," the boy said. "They're in my bag under my desk."

Time to head for Leith and the cinema on the top floor of the new complex at Ster Century. And, of course, when they got out of the car, having wound up four floors, they looked over the railing, the wind stiff in their faces, at the sun sparkling on the waters of the harbour and the sky above the distant coast of Fife high and cold and cloudless. It didn't matter, he'd given up on the zoo and the snow would be back before the afternoon ended.

They'd just missed a showing of *The Invincibles* and the next one wasn't until twenty past three. He found a phone and called home to leave a message on the answer machine for Liz. They ate fish and chips in the food hall in front of the vast windows looking out to Platinum Point, then wandered around from floor to floor, looking at the shops. Kerr went into Thomas Kincade, painter of light, and stood in front of paintings of chapels in mountain valleys and stagecoaches and sea harbours, settling at last in front of a gabled wooden house by a stream in what could only be called a dell. When the assistant joined them, Curle couldn't resist speculating, "If the door opened, would a man holding a bloodstained axe come out?" "Oh," the assistant said, "I shouldn't think so."

At one point, he finally got around to asking, "How are things? Everything all right at school?" Kerr muttered, "Fine," and he had no skill to get behind the suddenly veiled expression. Next moment the boy had hurried over to look through the glass down to where the royal yacht Britannia bobbed at anchor. "Can we go on it?" "Another time. The film's almost ready to start."

And so, after all, their stolen afternoon was spent in the dark.

When they came out, the evening light was washing out of the sky. They drove back talking about the picture they'd just seen and Kerr laughed a lot and explained bits to his father.

A police car was sitting outside the house when they arrived home.

As he opened the door, Liz swooped from the living room and gathered Kerr in her arms.

"Where have you been?" she cried at him over the boy's head.

Muffled against her chest, Kerr explained, "We saw *The Invincibles*. It was brilliant."

She said, "Upstairs. Come on, Kerr."

As Curle stood bewildered, Meldrum and McGuigan came from the room she'd left. The hall shrank with their arrival.

"What the hell's going on?" The tremor in his voice dismayed him.

It was McGuigan who answered. "Your neighbour Mrs Anderson got upset when she went to collect the children from school and Kerr wasn't there. Apparently she kicked up a fuss with the class teacher, and then phoned your wife. Who hit the panic button."

"But I phoned!" Curle led the way into the kitchen. The oval light at the side of the phone that should have shown a message had been recorded wasn't lit. "I don't understand." Trying to ignore their scepticism, he picked up the phone and pressed two. To his relief, the message he'd sent was there. He held out the phone so that they could hear his voice.

"I don't know why she panicked. She should have guessed he'd be with me."

"Have you taken him away for the afternoon before?" Meldrum asked.

He evaded the question. "Who else could it have been? She should have known."

"Maybe she did," McGuigan said. Why is he angry? Curle wondered. "Maybe she was afraid you were going to do something foolish."

"What?"

"Think about it," and he turned on his heels and left the kitchen. There was the sound of his feet mounting the stairs.

Curle made to follow. "I don't want him frightening my son."

"That's not his style," Meldrum said.

There was no sympathy in the harsh lines of the big man's face, but Curle found something reassuring in his calmness and the slow measure of his speech. He felt a firmness like granite, the ungivingness of a rock, and it was to that firmness he appealed.

"I feel as if he wants to arrest me."

"It's not up to him."

"You took away my clothes. Aren't there DNA tests? I didn't do it. I can give samples. Any kind of samples."

"There wasn't any semen," Meldrum said. "If that's what you're asking."

146

"What about Ali's blood? There must have been blood on him, the man who beat her."

"If we'd found blood on your clothes, you wouldn't be here."

Curle felt his legs weaken under him. He let himself sink into a chair at the table.

"All the same, your sergeant would lock me up if he could. It's personal. I know he feels like that." And he couldn't stop himself from finishing on a note of bathos. "It's — it's not professional, is it?"

"He has a strong moral sense. He's got no time for adulterers," Meldrum said. "He's not too keen on abortion either."

"For Christ's sake, is he too stupid to know there's a difference between adultery and murder?"

"He'd know that. He's pretty smart. Very smart actually. He won't be with me for long, he's a high flyer. The best detective sergeant I ever had." He paused. "Not that I've had much luck with detective sergeants."

As feet sounded on the stairs, Curle asked with a touch of desperation. "Why haven't you arrested me?"

Meldrum seemed to think before answering.

"An arrest changes things," he said. "It commits you to that being the truth of what happened. You can make it be the truth."

It didn't seem to bother him that McGuigan was behind him listening, his face set in a frown.

"It's best not to arrest someone until you are very sure," Meldrum said.

CHAPTER
TWENTY-NINE

Curle woke in the middle of the night and knew at once as if by instinct he was alone. Slowly after that, he made out the dim outline of the desk looming above him and realised he was in his study and then remembered reluctantly why he had been banished there. "Even in our worst times, I thought I knew you so well. Better than anyone in the world," Liz had said. "I don't know who you are any more." She'd spoken quietly, but then all their arguments for years had been like that. For Kerr's sake, they never shouted.

Misery kept him awake, but he must have escaped from it at some point for the next time he opened his eyes it was daylight. Determined not to get up until they had gone, for there was no way he could face either wife or son that morning, he lay listening for signs of activity. When at long last he heard the slam of the front door, he rolled off the couch and, gathering a blanket round him, padded over and pulled the curtain apart just wide enough to watch the car backing out of the drive.

He was in the kitchen making himself breakfast when the phone began ringing. He couldn't think of anyone he wanted to talk to. With the broken shell of the egg he'd just cracked into the pan dripping in his hand, he stared at it willing it to stop. Warily, when it didn't, he lifted it to his ear.

"Yes?"

"At last!"

"Jonah?"

"What were you doing, having a bath?"

"Having a pee."

"Anyway I got you. Didn't want you going out into the big world until I'd warned you."

"About what?" His stomach sank with fright.

"Have you seen a paper this morning?"

"No. I haven't been out of the house."

"You're in them. One of them at least."

"Tell me you're joking, for God's sake."

"Alice reads the *Sun*. Terrible thing for an intelligent woman to do. I tell her not to leave it lying about the office. She showed me it as soon as I walked in the door. And there you were. You took Kerr away for the afternoon, that right?"

"Is this a joke?" But how could Jonah know about Kerr being off school? "I take my son to the pictures and it's in the papers? My son played truant! That's the story?"

"When a detective inspector goes looking for him, I'm afraid it is. It's cleverly done. You have to hand it to them. It's done with a light touch, but the point's made. 'Detective Inspector Meldrum, who is investigating the brutal murder of a woman in Royal Circus, took time off apparently to check on the whereabouts of a schoolboy.' And not just any schoolboy — 'the son of well-known crime novelist Barclay Curle'. Whose novels, they mention in passing, feature a serial killer who kills women by beating them to death."

"Fuck."

"Fuck, indeed. They've got a photo of you too. Don't know where they got it, but it makes you look like Myra Hindley."

Half an hour later, he answered the doorbell to be met by two men, the one on the doorstep in his late forties smiling and holding out a copy of the morning paper folded to the page with Curle's photograph. It had been shot in close up from below with lighting that put a stare in his eyes and a touch of madness in his grin. Three or four years earlier, he'd been persuaded into the pose by a magazine photographer who fancied himself to be an artist. From his first sight of it, it had been an embarrassment.

"That photo's copyright," Curle said. "You'd no right to use it."

"Not the *Sun*," the man said, "the other one. We didn't think this was playing the game. Felt you might want to give your side of the story."

"There isn't a bloody story! I took my son to the pictures."

"It says here you came back to find DI Meldrum waiting for you. Is that right?"

Curle stared at him in silence.

"You must have thought that was a bit odd. Why do you think he was there?"

"My wife phoned for the police."

"She got herself a good one then. Look, can we talk inside?"

"No."

"Why give the neighbours an eyeful? For all you know, it was one of them gave the *Sun* a bell."

"I don't think so," he said without conviction.

"It's police harassment, isn't it? Get them off your back. Get it out in the open."

"I didn't say anything about harassment."

"Don't worry about wasting your time." The words tumbled out. "I'd make it quick. I know you're a busy man. Writing a book, are you? There's no such thing as bad publicity, isn't that what they say?"

As Curle began to close the door, the man stepped aside. Next moment, the one behind him had his camera up and the picture taken before Curle was out of sight.

And then the phone began ringing at regular intervals.

When it happened the first time, he picked it up and a voice he recognised said without preamble, "We could be talking five figures. And I can fix you up with a magazine deal that'll pay more."

After that he managed to ignore it for almost two hours.

When he cracked, he snatched up the phone and cursed into it.

"You've had the press in touch."

"Who is that?"

"DI Meldrum. What did they ask you?"

"Police harassment came up."

There was a silence. Then Meldrum asked, "Did you talk to them?"

"I'm not that stupid."

"Fine."

"Why would anyone want to tell the *Sun*? The reporter who doorstepped me thought it might have been a neighbour."

"No."

"Why not?"

"For the same reason it wasn't a teacher. You kept your son off school; who'd tell a paper? It had to be somebody who knew you were connected to Miss Fleming's death and knew about the boy being off."

The only person Curle could think of was DS McGuigan.

Meldrum let the silence run until Curle cleared his throat and said, "Anyway, I didn't talk to them."

"I can't tell you what to do, but it would be best if you didn't. I'm under enough pressure," Meldrum said.

CHAPTER
THIRTY

Another night spent on the couch in his study, another day in which he'd avoided speaking to his wife or son, another morning of lying staring at the ceiling until he was sure they'd left the house.

Penitent, he should have been on bread and water. Instead, when he managed to go into the kitchen at last, he was ravenous. He put three slices of bacon into the George Foreman, broke two eggs into the frying pan and made toast and coffee. As an afterthought, he washed half a dozen mushrooms and put them in beside the eggs. Sitting in a patch of sunlight at the kitchen table, he chomped his way steadily through everything on the plate, drank a second coffee and then a third and was settled in the front room, biliousness standing in for repentance, when the morning post clattered through the letterbox.

Shuffling through the usual bills and unsolicited offers of credit, he came on a plain white envelope and was shocked to recognise a handwriting he'd never expected to see again.

"I didn't know that you had a son. I read it in the paper this morning. And felt I had to write for the boy's sake. Not for yours; I'm still angry with you. I never thought I could forgive you and this isn't forgiveness. I don't think it is. I don't know what to call it. For the boy's sake I don't want you to come to any harm, not now, whatever you've done. Do you have other children? I always wanted a little girl of my own to care for. Children are precious, try to remember that, try to be good for your children's sake. Tie a millstone round their neck and throw them in the sea, that's what Christ would have done to those who make the little children suffer. People don't understand that Christ is fierce as well as gentle. Fierce and angry as well as gentle. Better for you not to forget that."

Like the others, it was signed *An Admirer*.

He turned the envelope in his hand and studied the postmark. It had been posted in Peebles. He was in no doubt that it had come from Martha Tilman. Was there a nursing home in Peebles? For some reason, he'd got the impression she'd been taken into care somewhere else. Would she have seen a morning paper there, wherever it was? And been in a position to write and post a letter quickly? And so he came full circle to the Peebles postmark. The more he thought about these things, the more he began to wonder if Joe Tilman had told them the truth.

Envelope in hand, he wandered like a caged beast from room to room. I'm under pressure, Meldrum had said. What else could he have meant than that he was under pressure to make an arrest? And if there was pressure, who could be applying it? There was only one obvious candidate: Assistant Chief Constable Fairbairn, Joe Tilman's brother-in-law. It was the only option that made sense. The rooms shrank as he paced and the walls closed in on him. Better do something, Curle decided, better do anything than wait for a knock on the door, an outstretched warrant, fists gripping his elbows, a hand steering his head down into the back of a police car.

Every writer understood the dangerous evocative power of images and yet, like a looped tape, helplessly he couldn't stop himself from running the vignette of his arrest as he drove from Edinburgh. In his distraction, he came into Peebles without recalling a foot of the road that had taken him there. Pulling himself together, he made his way with exaggerated care along the main street and up to Tilman's house on the crest of the hill. He drove past it on to a country road, turned in a farm gate and came back to park opposite the house, poised to return the way he'd come. Preparing my escape, he thought, like a robber parking outside a bank. He'd an image of himself fleeing the house with Tilman in pursuit.

When he rang the bell, however, it was a woman who answered. She was very pale, with blonde hair in lifeless straggles on either side of a thin face, but he recognised her as a shadow of the woman who'd stood smiling beside her sister, the two of them held like trophies between Tilman and Bob Fairbairn.

"I didn't ask you to come," Martha Tilman said, her eyes widening in recognition then staring over his shoulder as if at someone standing behind him.

"It was your husband I came to see."

"Why would you want to talk to my husband?" The question came sharply, taking him by surprise.

"I have some questions for him. About things he told me."

"You've met my husband?"

She sounded appalled.

"Only once." On some instinct, he added, "I wouldn't claim to know him. I'm not a friend of his."

After a moment of abstraction, she said politely, "Perhaps you'd better come in."

He followed her through the hall and along a short corridor. The room she led him into had a leather chair and a desk, a computer on a table and beside it a shelf of magazines. There were family photographs in matching frames hung on one wall, all featuring the same group, a man and woman with two blonde girls; some showed the girls as children, in others they were young and then older adults, as the sequence progressed the woman grew stouter, the man lost his hair: Martha Tilman, her sister and their parents. On a side wall, there was a painting of half a dozen tall languid flowers with feathery heads. As she perched on the desk seat and indicated he should take the comfortable chair, Curle assumed the room to be the one Tilman had described to Meldrum and himself as "just a place where she can be by herself".

"You won't tell my husband I wrote to you again? He made me promise not to send you any more letters."

"He won't find out from me. Can I speak to him?"

"He isn't here."

Was that true? Tilman's study was at the front of the house, but perhaps he'd been busy and left it to her to answer the doorbell. Perfectly possible that he was through there now, ubiquitous phone clutched to his ear negotiating some deal or other. Curle glanced uneasily at the door, which hadn't been closed properly and lay half-open. How would Tilman react if he found him here with his wife?

"You changed them from men to women," Martha Tilman said, breaking into his thoughts. "That was so wicked. Women have enough reason to be afraid."

But it was he who felt, if not fear, the sharp stab of discomfort. Physically timid, he'd always disliked the company of drunks, people not in control of themselves; how much worse the mad.

"I shouldn't have come," he said, hitching himself to the edge of the chair. "Don't upset yourself."

"Do you have a little girl?"

Shocked, he was silent; then, "No," he said grimly. At that moment, if a paper committing her to a mental home had been laid in front of him, he would have signed it.

"I always wanted a little girl. My mother had two little girls. When I'm told how much I resemble my mother, I always think but I have no children."

With a sigh, the tension went out of him. "I should be going." Then on impulse, he asked, "Why me? I haven't done anything you would have to forgive."

"If you can't see," she said.

Now all he wanted was to get away.

"You must have been at home," he said. "Yesterday, when you saw the article about me in the paper."

"It was delivered by mistake. We get the *Telegraph* and *The Times* and the *Herald*. Sometimes I look at them. I used to read a great deal. I loved Jane Austen, too . . . Now, not so much."

Don't tell me, he thought, now it's crime fiction. Nice to meet his target audience.

"When did you get home?"

She looked at him puzzled. "This is where I live."

"Yes, but I know you've been away."

She shook her head. "I don't go out much," she said in the same stilted, carefully formal tone.

Still he plodded on. In the moment, he told himself it was because he'd come all this way and should get something answered. Later, he would wonder if he had been trying to punish her for asking if he had a little girl.

"Your husband told me you had been away from home."

As startlingly as scaffolding collapsing on a city street, the façade broke apart. Her calmness, politeness, formality, restraint, even her moments of abstraction that must have been one more defence, smashed apart like ice in the boiling up of the fear and turmoil they had concealed.

"Is that what's going to happen? Is that what he's planned for me?" Her hands, as she stretched them out in appeal, shook uncontrollably. "Tell him you're not angry. Tell him I haven't written to you. Even if it's not true. Don't be angry." The last word faltered into a thin stretched moan: "Please."

He blurted out some kind of disclaimer, an apology, for what he wasn't sure, even a promise, the stream of words didn't matter, all he wanted was to get away from her distress.

As he got to his feet, however, she twisted down in her seat to open the bottom drawer of the desk.

"Take them!" she said, holding out to him at the full stretch of her arms a pair of shoes. She caught his hand and pressed one of the shoes into it. "Please!" she pleaded, pressing until his grip closed around it.

"You see?"

It was a court shoe, black leather soft under his fingers, heel a few inches high, nothing remarkable except for a long gash scored back from the toe. When he looked at the one she was holding, he saw that it was marked in the same way.

"Daddy had Mummy taken away. She died in that place. Even when I was little girl, I never believed she was mad. I never believed them. That made my aunt so angry she fetched these shoes. Look at them, she told me. Those marks were made when the men came and dragged your mother away."

As he made his escape along the hall, she came after him.

"Such cold people. My father and his sister. They were rich and they had power. Daddy could be so charming. They could make people do anything. Daddy could make the doctors do anything."

She gave a cry of pain and he had to stop himself from telling her to be quiet for fear her husband should hear them. He used both hands to get the door open, but once he was outside he found that he was still holding the shoe. He dropped it on the step and half ran down the path towards his car.

CHAPTER
THIRTY-ONE

He had been invited out to lunch yet again by Jonah, whom he'd seen more of in the last week than in a normal month or two. This didn't give him any kind of warm glow, since he put it down less to friendship than a love of gossip. As newspaper fodder, Curle, feeling a need to earn his keep, had shared the experience of that morning's expedition to Peebles.

"What were you thinking of?" Jonah wondered, spooning up a mouthful of tiramisu.

"It felt as if I was doing something. It was either that or sit at home."

"You could escape into your work."

As a man under suspicion of murder, Curle didn't dignify that with an answer.

"At least I found out that she wasn't away in some private hospital. She was at home. Why would Tilman have lied about that? And not just to me. To Meldrum, who's a policeman."

"People lie to policemen all the time."

"About how fast they've been driving."

"Well, he wasn't lying about a murder. This was before Ali Fleming was killed. You were there to complain that his wife had been sending you rude letters. There's no law says a man can't protect his wife — and if there is, there shouldn't be."

Moodily, Curle pushed his pudding away.

"I'm wondering if I should tell Meldrum."

"Why, in God's name, would you do that?"

"Isn't it obvious?"

"Not to me. Why unleash your detective on the poor woman, when she's clearly demented?"

"She wasn't in a hospital. She could have been in Edinburgh. You could say she's obsessed with murder. She's written to me about murdering people. All right, about murdering men — but she was angry with me for changing her men to women — so why shouldn't she change it, too, and choose a woman victim? And she's demented. Count that in as well."

Jonah made a face, "You don't believe any of that, do you?"

"It would give them something else to think of — apart from me."

"You're not really a nice man."

Curle sighed. "I don't like myself. Is that what you want to hear?"

Jonah set down his spoon. "I've lost my appetite, too."

"You've finished it!"

"Hmm. Want to go somewhere else? We could have a half pint and go on with this."

"I can't. It's Liz's day off, but there's a meeting of the pharmacists in charge of the shops in the group. I've sworn I'll be home for Kerr getting back from school."

"Your detective won't wear it, you know."

"Why not?"

"From what I've read, Ali Fleming was beaten to death. It must have been a man."

Curle shrugged. "Maybe she used a hammer." As soon as he'd said it, he felt sick. The words from his own mouth appalled him.

To hide his feelings, he spun the book lying beside Jonah's plate until he could decipher the title and author's name. "Another one? I can't keep up with him."

"Second this year. You know he's just been given an OBE?"

"Fuck!"

"Afraid so," said Jonah who'd been around writers too long not to share their pain at another's good fortune. "Think of it as an OBE for exports."

CHAPTER
THIRTY-TWO

"It's a silly idea," Kerr said.

"It's not mine," said Curle.

He'd been outlining to his son the concept of the pillow glove. It arose from the insight that the human animal was far from being ideal in construction. The list of faults might begin with the head, which was rather too large to slide comfortably through the birth canal. Later, the appendix, a trifling organ no bigger than a man's pinkie, was capable of causing agony, even death, despite having no useful function to perform. The bones of the back popped out at a stretch and a sneeze. Starting from scratch, what reasonably capable designer would have come up with teeth that decayed? All of which acted as preamble to the problem of finding a comfortable position for sleep with a limb attached at each of four corners. One of the best was to slide your arm under the pillow and rest your head on your upper arm as you slept. This, however, left the relevant hand and forearm poking out into what, in winter, might well be cold air. The answer was the pillow glove, a padded mitten that would cover fingertips to elbow.

Alone with his son at table, since Liz hadn't come home by dinnertime, Curle, feeling the need to make conversation, had outlined the conceit of the pillow glove, together with its theoretical underpinning, leaving out the problems of the birth canal.

"Whose idea was it?"

"Jonah's. You remember my agent? I took you in to see his office."

"Not recently."

"No. A while ago."

"I sleep on my front."

"He must sleep on his side, or the idea wouldn't have occurred to him, I suppose."

"If his arm gets cold, he should shut the window."

"I'll tell him that."

"I wonder what gave him the idea."

Curle laughed. "He sleeps alone."

To the best of his knowledge that had been true and still was. He had never heard Jonah so much as hint at anyone in his life. Naturally, he'd wondered if he might be gay, without ever catching any sign of it. It was possible that he had a secret mistress.

Smiling to himself as he ran over the married women Jonah knew, he gathered up plates, knives and forks and stacked them into the dishwasher. As he turned, he surprised Kerr biting his lip as he studied him.

"What is it?"

"It was cold last night."

Curle warily nodded agreement.

Avoiding his eye, Kerr observed, "You could have done with one of those things."

"Things?" No sooner had he spoken than he cursed himself, guessing what the answer had to be.

"One of those pillow gloves."

Later a number of things he might have replied occurred to him, among them the information that he too slept on his front, leaving unsaid the implication that he did so even when exiled out of the bedroom on to a couch in his study.

Instead, he asked brusquely, "Have you any homework? If not, you can watch television for a bit."

Three hours later when he was beginning the process of sending him to bed, Kerr asked, "When will Mum be home? Why is she so late?"

"I've no idea. I'll ask her when she comes in."

Liz didn't get back till almost ten o'clock, just after he had finally persuaded Kerr to go to bed. He heard tyres crunch on the gravel, the garage door go up and slam down, the key in the front door and was out in the hall, just happening to be on his way to the kitchen, as she came in.

"Kerr's in bed," he told her. "Maybe you want to say goodnight to him, before he goes to sleep."

"Of course I do," she said, "no maybe about it."

"I didn't mean —" What was the use?

He caught a trace of her perfume, one he'd bought her for Christmas, expensive, not one she wore every day. She was wearing a long Burberry-style raincoat and as she unbuttoned it, he saw under it the broad-shouldered jacket and the skirt that showed the plump sleekness of her thighs. What kind of meeting was it again? Did she always get dressed up to meet the

166

pharmacists from the other shops? He tried to remember, but the fact was he hadn't paid much attention.

"I'm just going up," she said.

"What about something to eat? I was going to make a sandwich."

"I'm not hungry."

"Have you eaten?"

"I've eaten," she said impatiently. "We went for a meal."

After the meeting? He was sure they hadn't done that before. Donald the owner had ten shops and three children. Maybe he'd added a child or a shop and taken them out to celebrate.

"Is that why you're so late?"

She gave him a glance and went upstairs, leaving the faint trace of her perfume lingering in the hall.

CHAPTER
THIRTY-THREE

The way it sometimes happens, everything fell into place the next morning. Before he'd got to breakfast, two things made Curle decide to check up on his wife that afternoon. The first was her announcement that she'd be late home.

"Thanks for letting me know," he said lifting his head from the pillow. He had a stiff neck from spending yet another night on the couch in his study. "Another meeting?"

"Don't be silly. Betty rang and asked if I wanted to meet her after work. I'm telling you in case you fret about where I am."

"So you want me to look after Kerr?"

"No need," she said. "He's having a sleepover with Graeme Anderson. His mother's collecting them both from school."

The information that he wouldn't be on call for Kerr made up his mind. He'd be there when the shop closed and follow her to see where she went, hopefully, almost definitely, though no longer certainly, straight home.

After breakfast he went into the study, switched on the computer and sat for a while staring at the single sentence he'd composed yesterday as the start of a new chapter. It was a nicely balanced sentence with an adjective like a ballerina poised on a noun solid as a rock, and an adverbial clause wagging its tail all the way to the full stop. He changed one "the" to an "a" and sat back well pleased. A little light as the total of a day's work, if you wanted to carp, but a nice sentence. After a while, he dozed off looking at it and woke up with a dry mouth needing a cup of coffee. I'm a murder suspect, he thought, and my wife is behaving oddly. Could Flaubert cope with that? I'll go into town and get a coffee there.

Normally, he would have taken the bus, but having decided this wasn't going to be an ordinary day, he backed his eight-year-old Vectra out of the garage. Fortunately, he wasn't a car buff; if he needed to make a show for someone, he borrowed Liz's.

Driving down through Morningside, he intended to use the park at the foot of Lothian Road. The heavy traffic, though, started him worrying in case he might have difficulty timing his arrival at Liz's shop at the end of the afternoon. Making up his mind, he crossed Princes Street and ran down to Stockbridge. There was a side street just outside the Zone where Liz parked her car; he knew about it because on occasion when he was in town he'd walk down to get a lift home from her. Mostly, it would have been more convenient for her to get a bus, but she had bitter memories of waiting at bus stops on winter evenings when she was a girl. He made a pass along the street without spotting the Subaru and was about to try the next street when impulse made him swing into a vacancy at the kerb. Parking places were so hard to come by in this city that taking one was almost a matter of instinct. It was early for lunch, but he could go for a walk and then find somewhere to eat.

He strolled to Inverleith Park and watched half a dozen Indian boys playing cricket. As he made his way back, a thin rain turned from harmless persistence into an intention to turn nasty. As the first big drops launched themselves, he dived down a stairway and took refuge in an Italian restaurant. Bean soup, veal, bitter coffee and a look at the morning paper, an hour and a half later he was back on the street, wondering how to kill time for the rest of the afternoon.

As he walked aimlessly, his feet led him out of habit to a familiar curve of buildings. He pressed the bell and waited until a woman's voice answered.

"It's Barclay Curle. I'd understand if you didn't want to talk to me."

"Come up."

Linda Fleming met him at the door of the flat.

"I'm glad you came," she said.

The warmth of her welcome took him by surprise. As he followed her along the passage into the front room, he caught the faintest trace of a perfume. Rich almost cloying, petals that hinted at their own decay, it was a scent he had despised himself for responding to so entirely. He had never asked for its name, but Ali had worn it all the time.

He took a seat in the room that had been so familiar and now seemed like part of another time, a lost world. He struggled as he had done before to find a resemblance between Linda Fleming and her dead sister. Something perhaps about the mouth, the shape of the eyes, but if there was one it was no greater than that between two people picked at random from a crowd in the street, strangers bred from the same Lowland stock. As she sat down and crossed her legs, he looked automatically at the curve of her calf and the sleek swell of her thighs. The red shirt she wore had the top buttons undone to show her breasts almost to the nipples and it seemed to him that her skirt was shorter than the one she'd worn to his house. She had struck him then as being restrained, modest even, if that wasn't too out of date a concept. He wondered if she had dressed for that first meeting to make some kind of statement about the difference between her and Ali. If so, what did the way she was dressed now mean?

"You came to the funeral," she said.

"I tried to stay well back. I hope no one was upset."

"Aunts and some people who had known my parents," she said dismissively.

"I was thinking of your parents. I wouldn't have wanted to upset them."

"No need, they weren't there. They live in Inverness now. My father's senile and my mother wouldn't leave him. He wouldn't understand."

Curle's quick imagination conjured up a picture of the old woman faced by the empty smile of her husband as the hour passed during which she knew her daughter was being buried far away. "How awful for her," he said.

"She's a strong woman. When my grandmother died, she didn't put up a stone over her grave. They'd quarrelled over something. Ali and I shared the cost of a stone as soon as we were independent. I can't tell you how angry she was with us for doing that. In a funny way, we almost welcomed her being so angry. If she ever felt much in the way of emotion normally, she never showed it. We were all glad to get out when our time came."

"What kind of man was your father?"

She stared at him. "Why would you want to know?"

"Ali never spoke about her parents."

"Why would she?" She cleared her throat. "Did she talk about me?"

He shook his head. She made a face, which might have been disappointment.

"A quiet man," she said. And when he looked puzzled, added, "My father. If it matters. Did you want him to be a monster?"

"Why would I have wanted that?"

"After Ali got involved with you, I read your books. You don't write about nice people."

He shrugged. "Books aren't life."

"You can't write books without giving something away."

"That's true." Goaded, he observed impulsively, "Ali had a dark side to her nature."

"Not with me," she said, her face frozen into a mask. "Not ever with me."

Scrambling to retrieve his mistake, he said, "I don't mean dark dark. Lovers' games. They don't count." What's said at night should be set aside in the morning.

"What did you talk about?"

Fucking. Being fucked. Power and submission.

He could find nothing to say, all the glib words deserted him. In the silence, he waited for her to condemn him.

"You might think we'd be remote from one another, given that upbringing," she said. "For some reason, it didn't work like that. All three of us loved one another. But she and I had time to get very close before Jean came along. Because there wasn't much affection around, she looked for it to me. There was only four years between us, but I felt like a mother to her. At least, I suppose that's how a mother would feel. I never had a child of my own."

Overt emotion always embarrassed him. For something to say, he asked, "Was Jean at the funeral?"

"Jean's dead. The youngest went first. She'd never been sick in her life. One morning, she felt unwell. From the diagnosis to the day of her death was only a matter of weeks."

Surreptitiously, he turned his wrist so that he could check his watch.

She caught the movement, however, and looking at her own watch cried, "Oh, it's time. Would you come with me?"

"Where?"

"He came down last night, but I told him it was late and I was going to have an early night. Then he invited me for tea today, since it's his afternoon off."

"Are we talking about Haskell?"

"Sorry," she said. "I'm not usually in such a muddle. Truth is, he gives me the creeps, just like Ali described.

If there was anything to be found out, I was determined to go. But I wasn't looking forward to it. And then you knocked at the door. The last person I expected to see. You have to come with me. It's like fate, you do see that?"

That explained the short skirt and the tight top, he thought. Did she imagine Bobbie Haskell would give himself away by grabbing a breast or sticking a hand up to see if she was wearing knickers? The shame that accompanied the thought (if she believed this fantasy that Haskell might have killed her sister, you couldn't deny her courage) weakened his resistance to going with her.

"He hasn't invited me," was the best he could do by way of protest.

"It doesn't matter," she said, picking up her handbag. "How would it look if he refused?"

CHAPTER
THIRTY-FOUR

The repetition of spaces undid Curle. While he had been with Linda Fleming, he had tuned out the colours, carpets, walls, the shape and position of furniture, the painting on the wall, things that reminded him of Ali in a room filled with memories. This repression had taken him through what could have been a very bad experience. In contrast, the similarity of the layout in Haskell's flat slipped effortlessly under his guard, despite everything in the room he now sat in being unlike anything in the one downstairs, so that for the first minutes after they were seated he had to struggle to keep his self-control.

"Biscuits all right?" Haskell asked, as he reappeared carrying a loaded tray. "I know Linda enjoys them with a cup of tea."

When he'd first met him, Curle had thought him no more than twenty. Now that seemed a mistake. With dark circles under his eyes, as if he hadn't been sleeping well, he seemed older.

"Isn't that a charming plate?" Linda Fleming asked as Curle picked a biscuit from it.

It seemed to him a perfectly ordinary plate with a blue border, but he wasn't interested in such things.

"You have lovely taste," she said to Haskell. "He chose all the furniture," she informed Curle, "and worked out the colour scheme."

"It's nice," Curle managed, looking around vaguely.

"I offered to help Ali, you know," Haskell said. "She would talk about getting her flat redecorated, but she never actually got round to it. I told her, you could make this place a jewel."

Little fucking gay decorator, Curle thought. She won't ever get round to it now. He was embarrassed by the sting of tears.

Blinking and looking round again, he said flatly, "Like this."

For what seemed an interminable time, the two discussed decoration and furnishings while Curle ate biscuits, one after another, absent-mindedly, washing them down with weak coffee.

"I'd even have painted the ceiling for her," Haskell said. "I could have got men in, but I did this myself." And over the woman's responsive murmurs, "I've always been good with my hands."

After a time, Linda Fleming said, "I have to go to the loo."

"I'll show you," Haskell said getting up

"No need! I suppose it's where Ali's was?"

She had no sooner left the room than Haskell asked, "Am I being stupid?"

Curle, startled by the abruptness of the question, was at a loss.

"Sorry?"

"I know something was muttered when you arrived, but, I'm sorry, I have no idea why you would be visiting Linda."

"To see if she was all right?" The younger man's assumption of a right to question him offended Curle. "I haven't seen her since the funeral."

It was Haskell's turn to seem disconcerted.

"You mean Ali's funeral?" Curle didn't think that deserved an answer. Who fucking else's? he wondered. "You were at Ali's funeral? I'd have gone if I'd known where it was."

"You should have asked."

Haskell jumped up as if he was going to walk out, but instead began to pace about the room.

"Who was there?" he asked.

"Relatives."

"I can't imagine you being welcome. Do you mind me being honest?"

"Yes. I mind a good deal."

"You must have cared for her." He sat down again and regarded Curle solemnly. "I give you credit for that."

Curle, a man normally timid about violence, had a strong impulse to get up and punch the young fool in the mouth.

"If I could be honest with you," he said, "I don't give a fuck what you give me credit for."

"All the same, it's true." Although Haskell's cheeks had flushed, his voice was quieter, so soft that Curle strained to catch his words. "I thought you were just using her. God knows how many women he has on the side, that's what I thought. Adultery means nothing now, it's just a word. It made me so angry that she would let herself be treated like that."

"Angry with her?" No sooner were the words out of his mouth than Curle had a vision of how Ali had died, the image Brian Todd had described to him of her being beaten to a pulp.

"Not with her!" Haskell cried. "I was her friend. Angry with you, I'm not trying to deny that. I told you so, didn't I?"

Sick of the conversation and of the blond man's histrionics, Curle wanted nothing more than to get out.

He must have glanced at the door to the hall, for Haskell turned his head towards it and frowned.

"She's a long time," he said. "Perhaps I should knock?"

Before he could move, however, the door opened to admit Linda Fleming back into the room.

She hurried with short steps back to her chair. As she settled herself, she seemed unaware of how far the short skirt rode up her thighs. There was, too, a slight flush on her cheeks. Perhaps, Curle thought, taking so long embarrasses her. In a moment, however, as she straightened from putting her bag on the floor beside her chair, she pulled the skirt down and asked, "What did I miss?"

"I was saying," Haskell said quickly, "how sorry I am not to have been at the funeral. I could have asked for time off. Perhaps if you tell me where she's buried, I could take flowers to the grave."

Her face froze for a long moment before she managed to speak. "The funeral was in Glasgow. Too far to ask you to go."

"I was her friend," he said reproachfully.

Despite Curle's efforts, it took another quarter of an hour before they left. Linda Fleming, perversely, as it seemed to him, taking her time about their departure.

At the door, Haskell laid a hand on her arm.

"Take a deep breath."

He smiled at her bewilderment.

"Don't tell me you can't smell it?"

As he spoke, Curle caught the heavy mouth-watering smell and was amazed not to have noticed it before, a sign of how tense he had been when they arrived.

"What is it?" Curle asked.

Haskell flicked him a glance, but spoke to the woman. "Ghisau — Sardinian beef stew. I made it once for Ali. I get the beef from Colin Peat, a butcher in Haddington. It's every bit as good as the Sardo Modicano the Sardinians use. And the best plum tomatoes I could find, though they're not San Marzano unfortunately."

"I'm sure it's very nice," Linda Fleming said. His hand still lay on her arm.

"Come and help me eat it. There's far too much for one. I can freeze what's left, but I'd much rather enjoy it with someone. I was going to eat about seven. Please come."

"I can't," she said. "I'd like to, but Mr Curle has asked me to eat with him."

At Haskell's glance, Curle nodded.

A moment later, the door was closed on them.

As they went down the stair, Curle said, "I don't think he cares much for me."

She didn't answer, hurrying down so quickly he feared she would stumble. As they came to her door and he began to say goodbye, she urged, "Come in! Quickly!" glancing at the stair to the upper floor as if expecting pursuit.

Reluctantly, he followed her inside.

"I'm sorry," he said, "but I really have to be going. I've arranged to meet my wife."

Disregarding his words, she beckoned him into the front room. As he followed, she was upending her handbag on to the small coffee table. A fat grey notebook tumbled out of it.

"I found it in his bedroom," she said. "It was in the drawer of a bedside table. I think it's his diary."

"Oh, Christ!" Curle said.

CHAPTER
THIRTY-FIVE

Walking away from Royal Circus, Curle could still feel in his chest a physical memory of how his heart had pounded as he came from what he still thought of as Ali's flat out on to the landing. He'd fully expected to confront Haskell demanding the return of his stolen property. Going down the stairs to the street had been a flight from the risk of pursuing footsteps. It shows what a bad conscience does, he consoled himself, when even a weed like Haskell can put the wind up you. To make matters worse, Linda Fleming's impulsive theft of the book had been pointless. A hasty glance had told her it was a diary, but they'd read it from end to end and found nothing more incriminating than dental appointments and books ordered on Amazon.

Curle was almost back to his car, when he stopped abruptly and crossed the road to check the numberplate of a green Subaru estate parked under a streetlight. He wondered how he'd missed it earlier. Perhaps Liz had for some reason needed to use the car in the afternoon and found this place when she came back. In any case, she'd parked facing against the traffic. He went back to his own car and angled the driver's side mirror so that he could just glimpse the Subaru. She would have to come right across the road, giving him a good chance of spotting her and making it easy to pull out himself and follow. A glance at his watch told him that it was just after six.

As he waited, he wondered what would happen when Haskell realised his diary was missing. It might not happen for some time, for he didn't seem to make much use of it. If they were lucky and a week or two passed, maybe even longer, it was just possible that he might not connect its disappearance with his two visitors. Nice to believe that, but Curle didn't persuade himself. Wishful thinking, he thought, biting his lip. For one thing, he had a feeling Haskell didn't entertain many people to his flat. On the worst scenario, he'd notice it was missing this evening, in which case he'd know at once who had taken it. Entirely absorbed in her disappointment that the diary proved nothing, Linda Fleming had seemed surprisingly unconcerned about the consequences of her action, but he should have stayed with her longer. Brooding on this, he almost missed the Subaru looming into his mirror as it cut across the traffic.

By the time he managed to pull out, he was three cars behind it. It was harder to follow a car than he had realised. All right in fiction, in real life it would involve a team of pursuers and more than one car. Twice, the Subaru went through a set of lights, which caught him on the red. By good luck more than skill, he reeled her back into sight each time. It was quickly obvious that she wasn't going home, and when they turned right on to Corstorphine Road he fretted himself with the

182

notion that she might be on her way to Glasgow. She was at least as able a driver as he was, and he wouldn't be able to keep up with the Subaru on the motorway. They passed the zoo and a light, steady rain began to fall. It was a relief when she turned into a side road. Not long afterwards, her indicator lights came on. As he drove past, he saw the neon sign indicating a hotel.

He parked and walked back, hunching his shoulders against the rain. Squinting between a pair of stone pillars, he saw the Subaru at the end of a line of half a dozen cars parked in front of the façade of a long two-storey red-brick building. Reluctantly, like a man going to be hanged, he made for the splash of light that marked the entrance.

On the other side of the revolving doors, it was dry and warm. A woman looked up from her place behind the reception desk, studying him as he hesitated. Through an open door behind her a man in shirtsleeves could be seen talking on the phone.

From his left, he heard what might have been voices coming from what he assumed was a bar. As he went nearer, however, the sound resolved into a fretful Muzak track, and the dimly lit space was empty except for a couple seated at a table in the far corner. Their heads were close as they leaned towards one another. Curle recognised Brian Todd at once, but it was only when he lifted his glass and said something that made the woman laugh that he was forced to admit the woman was Liz. In a state of shock, he retreated across the hall under the watchful eyes of the woman behind the desk. The whole thing had taken less than five minutes.

He sat in the car and watched the rain run down the window until the glass fogged over. At some point, he switched on the engine. Later he turned it off again. There wasn't any question of driving away. It would have helped if he could have felt angry instead of hopelessly sad. Hopefully, anger might come if the wrong word was said. He couldn't generate it from inside himself. There were stock responses to situations like this. From old habit, he ran little playlets in his mind. Those men were lucky who manufactured an image of themselves to live by: *I can't help my temper, I don't take any crap, My father could do it with a look, I'd kill her if she ever.* Sceptical of graven images, for every situation in his life he had to invent who he was. Amid all the flux, the only certainty was that he couldn't drive away. To drive away, he would have had to be someone else.

He walked back to the hotel through the slanting rain. When he came to the pillars, it came into his head that he couldn't remember locking the car as he got out. He stood for a moment thinking about it, then went on towards the entrance. The Subaru was parked where it had been before.

There was still a couple in the bar, an Asian girl and an older white man at a different table. As he turned away, he saw a sign for the dining room. Ignoring the intent gaze of the woman behind the reception desk, he went across and down a short corridor lined with red and gold wallpaper. The dining room was spacious and

184

the tables had white cloths, place settings and wineglasses, spirals of folded napkins. It looked like a pleasant place to eat, though there was no telling about the food since there were no diners. As he looked round, a waiter appeared and approached him menu in hand. He explained that he was looking for two friends who'd been in the bar earlier. No one was booked for dinner, the waiter assured him.

Back at reception, the woman denied any knowledge of the couple he described.

"Their car's still outside," he said. "And they're not in the bar or the dining room."

"Some people like to eat in their room."

"Is that what they're doing?"

"I told you," she said, blank faced, "I don't know who you're talking about."

Outside, the rain was heavier, settling in for a wet night. He plodded through it to the car. It was locked, so that was all right.

When he came in out of the night for the third time, the woman narrowed her eyes at him and frowned.

"I need a room," he told her.

She stared at him without answering.

"My car won't start. I'll phone the AA in the morning."

"I could phone them for you now."

"It's wet. I'm soaked. I'm tired. I want a room," he said. "Isn't that the business you're in?"

Once he had the key in his hand, he couldn't resist saying. "Maybe I'll see my friends at breakfast."

"Seven-thirty till nine-thirty. If you want it earlier than that, let us know before ten this evening."

She spoke without looking at him, studying some spot just above his left shoulder, and turned away.

In the room, he sat on the chair by the bed without taking his coat off. He could always, he thought, go from door to door listening for the creaking of bedsprings. It didn't seem a plan likely to work. After a while, he phoned room service and ordered scrambled eggs, toast and coffee. The waiter who pushed the trolley in, a youth with acne virulent enough to put Curle, a sensitive soul, off his food, was a blank wall to questions about who else might be taking meals in their rooms. It made Curle wonder if discretion had to be a speciality of a hotel catering for adulterers. Or maybe Todd was a big tipper.

CHAPTER
THIRTY-SIX

The woman was tired to the bone. It had been a hard day. She had sat down just for a moment intending to get up and finish the meal on the tray as a kind of supper before going to bed. Her eyes had closed and opened and closed again and she had slept. As she slept, her eyelids flickered and there had been some kind of dream. She had moaned a little and moved her head from side to side. One hand came up and stroked the silver chain around her neck. From the expression on her face, the watcher had been unable to tell if the dream was about sex or fear or the falling dream that everyone experienced as the sleeping heart missed a beat. It might have been set in her past or present or some place outside time. As she opened her eyes, the watcher had the impulse to ask her what it had been. He didn't, though, and even if he had thought better of that a moment or two afterwards, it would have been too late, of course, since even so brief an interval of time would have dissipated the dream like a handful of smoke, which was a pity since it was the last dream she would ever have.

The strange thing was that when she opened her eyes and saw the blurred shape of a man's head against the light, as it might have been of a husband or father or lover, she stretched out her hand with a gentle startled expression as if to touch his cheek. The gesture frightened him so that he ducked away, fast as a boxer avoiding a blow. The violence of the movement brought her to her senses. Her mouth flew open, but instead of a scream or a cry for help, she gave a harsh unbroken seemingly endless gasp as he crushed her throat with both hands. Arms, legs, the trunk of her body, flailed and spasmed as she fought against him, making the shapes of someone falling until at last her heart stopped and she lay still.

CHAPTER
THIRTY-SEVEN

As he woke, Curle reached for the warmth of a woman by his side, hand flexed as if to lift the weight of a breast. The space beside him was cold. It took him a moment or two to remember where he was. He rolled out of bed and pulled on his trousers and shirt. The red numbers on the bedside radio told him it was four in the morning. Room key in hand he went down through the silent hotel and out to the front steps. The Subaru was still there.

At seven he went down and checked again, then walked around the streets till half past when the dining room opened. He sat toying with cereal and pushing eggs and bacon round the plate till the fat congealed. He ordered more toast and drank coffee as people came and went. At half eight he went out again to check the cars parked outside. The Subaru was gone.

Sitting in the car, chilled from being parked in the open all night, he dialled Jonah's number and let it ring till he was sure there would be no answer. Without much hope, he tried the office and was surprised when Alice, the PA, put him through.

"You're in early."

"Things to do," Jonah said. "What do you want?"

"The home address of Brian Todd."

There was a long pause. "What makes you think I would have it?"

"I have faith in you. That and the fact I can't think of anyone else to ask."

"Have you looked in the phone book?"

"I'm not at home. Don't ask."

Jonah grunted. After another pause, shorter this time, he said, "Give me a minute."

Getting the address had been an avoidance measure. Once he had it, there was nothing between him and the problem. What was he going to do? At some point, he'd have to go home, though he wasn't sure what the word meant any more. Kerr would be back later after school and this was one of Liz's afternoons at work. He supposed, despite everything, she would have gone to work this morning. Did Brian Todd have any children? He decided to go and find out.

As he stopped at a cash machine to refill his empty billfold, his uncontrollable imagination conjured an image of his wife trailing the faint unmistakable scent of fish around the pharmacy. What was that old story about women who herded together synchronising their periods? The entire staff of the pharmacy would be on heat. That manner of thinking did no justice to how bad he felt, but the habit of it was too old to break.

The address he'd been given was in Barnton, a substantial house on a corner site with cherry trees, winter skeletal, behind the hedge on either side of the path that led to the front door.

The bell was answered on the third ring.

"Yes?" She looked startled as if she'd been expecting a familiar face.

"I wonder if I could speak to Brian?"

"My husband's at work." A man and woman apparently arguing together sounded from behind her until they were drowned in music. Since it seemed unlikely she had an orchestra in her front room, it was probably a radio.

"I'm a friend of his."

"Ye-es?" Without thinking about it, he'd assumed Todd would have a trophy wife, one of those heads of long blonde hair and white wet teeth that would look handsome mounted on a plaque on the wall. This woman had a face the size and colour of a little linen handkerchief with high cheekbones and a pointed chin. The teeth were white enough but they pressed against her mouth as if there was too little skin on her face. Standing with arms clasped tight around her as if for warmth, she had the look of an anorexic.

"We were at school together," Curle said.

"Oh, yes."

"Maybe you could tell him I called." Give the bastard something to think about. It was better than nothing. "My name is Barclay Curle."

To his astonishment, she broke into a wide smile. "Not the book writer?" And at his nod, she stepped back and asked him inside.

As they sat down in the living room on fat armchairs that could have seated two people and left space for a midget, she explained, "I spend a lot of my time

191

reading. I love detective stories. Your Doug Kirk is a particular favourite."

He sat boorishly silent. All the stock responses he'd evolved to meet that kind of statement deserted him. He stared at the big close-ups of heads mouthing on the television screen. She'd put the sound off when they came into the room, but left the set on.

"My name's Pat, but I expect you know that."

"Brian's spoken of you," he lied.

"I don't know why he never said to me."

A memory stirred of Todd claiming to have heard of Mae's death from some article read to him by his wife.

"You didn't know we knew one another?"

The little face broke into a smile again. Vivaciously, she said, "He can be terrible like that. And you were at school together!"

"We lost touch."

"It's so easy to do that. I had so many friends and . . ." She trailed off, then looked up and said brightly, "it's so easy to do that."

When she said that, something clicked in his mind like the slotting into place of a jigsaw puzzle piece.

"Brian's a sociable man," he said. "These last few weeks I've come across him all over the place. Does he bring many people home?"

Her lips pulled apart, but she didn't speak, just stared with a fixed frozen little smile.

"Home for dinner, I mean. My wife and I don't have many dinner parties, but that's my fault. I don't like entertaining. Does Brian like entertaining?"

She shook her head.

192

"You surprise me. He's so sociable in company. Maybe he's different at home. Some people are like that. One thing outside, and somebody different at home. Is Brian like that, different at home?"

"He's very busy," she said quietly.

"That must be lonely for you." And before she could answer, he went on, "But maybe you have a job? My wife works, which is another reason we don't have people to the house much. Do you work?"

"No."

"You must be lonely."

"I read," she said.

"And watch television in the morning."

Her eyes slid to the set in the corner.

"You should think about finding a job. It would get you out of the house," he said. "But maybe Brian wouldn't like that?"

Suddenly he sickened of what he was doing. He wasn't a bully, and he despised himself for what she had drawn out of him.

He waited for her to look back at him so that he could apologise and get out of there, but she kept watching the television, so intently she might have been making up dialogue in her head to match the faces on the screen.

CHAPTER
THIRTY-EIGHT

LINDA FLEMING: That poor woman! Is it true she was killed last night?

DS McGUIGAN: You were at home then. Are you sure you didn't hear anything?

LINDA FLEMING: That means she lay all day today. Lying there alone, the way Ali did. It's a nightmare. She could have been there for weeks. I had the impression no one ever visited her.

DS McGUIGAN: And last night, you didn't hear anything unusual?

LINDA FLEMING: Sounds of a struggle, you mean?

DS McGUIGAN: Somebody shouting. Maybe a scream.

LINDA FLEMING: My flat is above hers. You should ask the people below her, on the ground floor. They might have heard noises, the way it happened with my sister.

DS McGUIGAN: We don't think there was a struggle.

DI MELDRUM: (cutting in) It's too early to say what happened.

LINDA FLEMING: I know how she died. I saw her. (Voice breaking) I saw her poor body.

DI MELDRUM: I'm sorry that happened.

LINDA FLEMING: It wasn't by accident. Don't you understand? He meant me to see her. That's why he asked me to come with him. He wanted me to see what he'd done. I've told you what my sister said about him. I should have told you before. For God's sake, why don't you arrest him before someone else is killed?

DI MELDRUM: I'm sorry, we don't have any evidence that would let us do that.

DI MELDRUM: I'm not clear on this. Explain to me why you asked Miss Fleming to go with you into the flat.

BOBBIE HASKELL: I'm just a neighbour. I'm not a policeman. I'd have thought it was obvious. I couldn't go into a woman's flat uninvited all on my own.

DI MELDRUM: Why ask Miss Fleming?

BOBBIE HASKELL: Why not?

DI MELDRUM: Her sister had been murdered. I wouldn't have thought she was the obvious person to ask.

BOBBIE HASKELL: I see that. Oh, dear. All I can say is I didn't think. If my mother was still alive, she'd say, that's the trouble with you Bobbie, you *don't* think.

DS McGUIGAN: Come to that, why did you go in at all?

BOBBIE HASKELL: I saw that the door was open. I came home from work, and as I was going upstairs I saw that her door was open. Just an inch or so, but it meant anybody could walk in. I pushed it back a little more and I saw that the two locks were off. The policeman later told me that they could have been like that since the murder. Maybe the draught from the street door when I came home pushed it a little open.

DS McGUIGAN: Do you always go in somewhere because the door's open?

BOBBIE HASKELL: Of course not! But I knocked and got no answer. I couldn't think where she'd be. And she wasn't a stranger, she was a friend of mine. I felt responsible for her. I'm sure you feel responsibility for your friends. It's natural, isn't it?

DI MELDRUM: You're claiming that Eva Johanson and you were friends?

196

BOBBIE HASKELL: But of course we were. Never a week went by without us having a chat. Just a word or two, if we met on the stair. Though sometimes we'd have a coffee, once or twice in my flat, but mostly in hers — when I was lending a hand with something.

DI MELDRUM: Electrical repairs, that kind of thing? DIY jobs? I remember you told us you were good with your hands.

BOBBIE HASKELL: Always have been. My mother boasted about that to our neighbours.

DI MELDRUM: Yet when we interviewed Eva Johanson, she told us she didn't even know your name.

BOBBIE HASKELL: . . . That surprises me . . . But I know why.

DI MELDRUM: You do?

BOBBIE HASKELL: She was an old lady.

DI MELDRUM: Not all that old. In her late fifties.

BOBBIE HASKELL: But things had changed so much for her with her husband's death. Not certifiable. I don't mean she could have been sectioned, isn't that what you call it? But she'd lost her grip. You must have noticed that. She was terribly lonely.

197

DI MELDRUM: (sceptical) She didn't remember your name because she was lonely?

BOBBIE HASKELL: *And* she'd just had a terrible shock. I mean she saw the body! That young constable who got into Ali's flat shouldn't have let her follow him in, should he? Poor thing! If Ali's body was anything like what we saw last night, I'm surprised she was able to remember her own name. (Voice rising) When are you going to stop these horrors? For God's sake, there's an obvious suspect!

CHAPTER
THIRTY-NINE

"I'm sorry," Curle said.

"It was an odd reaction," Meldrum said. "You're the first person who ever smiled when I told them someone was dead."

"I wouldn't call it a smile. It didn't feel like a smile. The truth is I was relieved."

McGuigan asked sharply, "Relieved?"

"When you said someone had been murdered, I thought you were going to say Linda Fleming."

"So you smiled?" McGuigan sounded incredulous. "Are you saying you wanted to hear Linda Fleming was dead?"

"No! That's not what I said. Don't twist what I said!"

"Don't get excited," Meldrum said quietly. "Your wife will wonder what's happening."

Oh God, Curle thought, and my son, my son's upstairs. Softly he said, "I didn't want anyone dead."

"What was that?" McGuigan asked. "You'll need to speak louder."

"What made you think it might be Linda Fleming who'd been murdered?" Meldrum asked, himself speaking softly.

"Have you spoken to her?"

The two detectives studied him in silence.

"I saw her yesterday afternoon," Curle said. "She asked me to go up to Haskell's room with her."

"You went to see Linda Fleming yesterday afternoon?" McGuigan asked. "Why would you do that?"

"Because I'd unfinished business with her. Because I went to Ali's funeral." He looked at Meldrum. "You saw me there. And I wanted to tell her sister what I didn't get a chance to say then. How sorry I was about Ali. That was all. But I was no sooner in the door than she started about Haskell being the one who had killed her. And then she said he'd asked her up for coffee, and would I go with her? If I hadn't been there, I'm sure she'd have gone alone, even though she was afraid of him. She's determined to find her sister's killer."

"So she talks to you?" McGuigan said dubiously.

"Because she knows I would never have harmed Ali! She's sure Haskell did it. She must have told you that. Why else would she have taken the diary?

"What diary?" Meldrum asked.

"When we were in Haskell's flat, she made an excuse about having to use the lavatory. But while she was away, she looked in his bedroom and took a diary she found. She showed it to me when we got out of there. I told her how foolish she'd been."

"She didn't say anything about that to us."

"Because there wasn't anything in it," Curle said. "Just dates with his dentist, stuff like that. God knows what she thought she'd find. A description of committing the murder, I suppose. It was just madness.

But when you said someone had been murdered, my first thought was that Haskell had found his diary was missing."

"This is the diary that had nothing in it?" McGuigan asked.

"But it still meant she suspected him!"

McGuigan shook his head as if human foolishness never ceased to amaze him. "It's a bit far-fetched, isn't it? I can't see anyone committing murder over a diary of dental appointments. In any case, we're not here about Linda Fleming. Mrs Johanson was the one killed last night. And it wasn't anything to smile about."

Curle made a gesture of protest, looking to Meldrum as if for help. Meldrum, however, did not meet his glance.

"Would you explain to us again where you were last night, sir?" McGuigan asked.

CHAPTER
FORTY

Curle was sitting over the remnants of his breakfast when he heard the outside door being opened. A moment later, Liz came into the kitchen.

"What's wrong?"

"Nothing." She pulled out a seat on the other side of the table and sat down.

"Kerr's gone to school?"

"Yes!" She made a gesture of impatience. For once, it seemed that didn't matter.

He sat in silence taking her in. She had left her coat in the hall or the car. She had on a dark grey skirt and a white blouse, the outfit she wore to work. He saw that she was wearing her hair longer, almost to the shoulders, dark almost black hair, thick and shining from regular brushing. She was tall, almost as tall as he was, with long legs and finely shaped breasts pressing against the fabric of the white blouse. She had a strong face, the nose a little large, the mouth wide, not pretty at all, handsome perhaps, you couldn't be in any doubt looking at her that she was intelligent. It seemed as if he was seeing her properly, really looking at her, as he hadn't done since Mae had been killed. There had been a time when he had loved her more than anyone in the world.

"I'm so sorry," she said.

"What would that be for?"

"For not being here when you needed me."

"To give me an alibi? You think I need one? Anyway, you told them I was here all night. I appreciate that. You lied for me."

"It wasn't a lie! I know you were here. Where else would you be?"

"Question is, where were you?"

"You don't need to believe this, but when I woke up yesterday morning I was worried about you. I imagined you going crazy when I didn't come home. I thought, he'll have phoned the hospitals. I thought you'd have phoned the police." She stopped abruptly. "You didn't phone the police?"

"No."

"Thank God for that."

"So where exactly would that be, where you woke up yesterday?"

She put her hand over her mouth. Her eyes above it seemed enormous.

"I woke up in a hotel bedroom. I can't believe I'm saying that."

"Alone?"

"Yes. A place called the Smiddy, over by the zoo. There wasn't anything wrong with it. I mean, it wasn't squalid or anything, just an ordinary hotel room in an ordinary hotel."

"I wish you'd take your hand away from your mouth. It's what liars do, cover their mouths."

Somewhere under the surface he felt surprise when she did it. She wasn't a meek woman. Her submissiveness fed his anger unreasonably.

She brushed at her face as if unconsciously clearing away strands of fog. "It was dark and at first I didn't know where I was, and when I did it was hard to believe. I got up when it grew light and sat in a chair. I went to work because I couldn't think of anything else to do. I was still wearing the clothes I'd worn to the shop the day before. I couldn't face coming home."

"Home," he said, and felt his mouth twist as if he were going to have a stroke.

"We've been angry with one another for so long. But when I learned about your mistress, I wasn't angry. It was all mixed up with her being killed. How could you be angry with someone who was dead? I wasn't angry, I was ashamed. When he asked me to dinner, that was all it was supposed to be."

"In a hotel?" he asked bitterly. And then he realised that he hadn't asked the obvious question. Hadn't asked because he knew the answer. "Who the hell are we talking about?"

"Brian Todd."

"That bastard." Anyone in the world but that bastard.

"He was kind. He seemed kind. He'd come to the shop and taken me to lunch. He talked about you, when you were at school together. What a swine he'd been. How he wished that he could go back and be different. He'd read your books. He admired you. I needed someone to talk to about how I felt. And he understood that. And then he asked me to dinner and Kerr was away, there wasn't anything to take me home. I said yes."

"And then you went to bed with him."

"He'd booked a room. I could have walked out, but you've no idea how natural he made it seem."

"You've got that right. I've no idea."

"We went up to the room. He'd got them to send up a bottle of champagne in an ice bucket. I took off my clothes and then I went to the bathroom. When I came out, he'd put his jacket back on. I was standing there naked, and he had his coat over his arm. He looked me up and down slowly and then he said, 'Enjoy the champagne.' "

He knew it was true and almost choked on the fury of his anger with her.

"You stupid, stupid bitch. It wasn't about you. He did it to hurt me. Were you too stupid to know that?"

She put her hand over her mouth and took it away at once as if not wanting to offend him.

In a voice almost too quiet for him to hear, she said, "I didn't kill Mae. You've never stopped blaming me. Why do you blame me?"

It was then he felt something in his chest, some old barrier, shatter into pieces that would never be put together again. As he shook his head helplessly over and over again in denial, tears poured down his cheeks.

CHAPTER
FORTY-ONE

It was coming to the time of year when he wouldn't fill the nut holder any more. Held by a length of twine, it hung from a branch of the tree in the garden and during the months after Christmas there would always be little birds dabbing at the nuts with their blunt beaks, right way up, or like acrobats head down. Some woman neighbour had told him, talking from a ladder as she sawed off a branch intruding over her fence, that once you started feeding the birds you had to do it all year round. It's become one of their food supplies, she'd said. It seemed to him, though, that if birds couldn't forage for themselves in the summer something was wrong. He got a good feeling from doing a kind deed in the winter, but filling the holder all summer would make him feel as if they were taking him for some kind of fool.

At the moment, though, after the emotional storm with Liz, who had taken refuge from it all by going into work, feeding the birds was soothingly mindless. He stood on the bench and unhooked the holder from the tree branch. From the garden hut, he fetched the plastic Tesco bag full of nuts that hung on a hook behind the door. He'd set the holder upright on the slats of the bench and now he lifted the cap off and started to pour in handfuls of peanuts. When it was almost filled, he got down on hands and knees and gathered as many as he could of the nuts that had fallen through the slats, on the theory that feeding birds was fine, but feeding vermin was a bad idea.

It was like that, down on hands and knees, that he heard the garden gate bang back against the fence. His first thought was that it couldn't have been properly fastened, his second that there was no wind to blow it open. He looked over his shoulder and saw Brian Todd striding towards him.

"You cunt!" His face red to match the colour of his hair, the shouting was instant and combustible. In a long Crombie coat, seen from below he seemed like a square of darkness blotting out the sky.

Curle scrambled up, but as he got to his feet a hand in his chest sent him staggering back.

"How dare you?" The tirade continued on a single breath. "How fucking dare you? What the hell did you think you were doing?"

In a state of shock, Curle opened and closed his mouth, not able to speak or make any response. After it was over, though in his heart he knew a better man would have met anger with anger, he would try to comfort himself that it had all been too sudden.

Rage seemed to have congested Todd's face, laid thick strips of flesh around the eyes and mouth. Flecks of spittle gathered at the corners of his lips.

Curle had no doubt the man was out of control and was about to attack him with his fists.

"I should beat the shit out of you!" he screamed, the swollen face inches from his victim.

At that moment, from the other side of the six-foot wooden fence, a clear voice floated up like a blessing from an unseen neighbour. "Is something wrong?"

Todd leaned even closer and whispered, "Things never change, do they? That bitch Harriet Strang at school. And you're still hiding behind a woman's skirts."

"Is something wrong, Barclay? Should I call the police?"

Curle found his voice. He called, "It's all right, Jill. He's just going."

Todd took a half step backwards. In a conversational voice, which somehow made worse the fierceness of his words, he said, "Don't come to my house again or I'll hurt you. My wife is out of bounds, understand?" He poked Curle in the chest, three times for emphasis. "Don't you ever, ever, ever, speak to her again."

He turned as if to go, but then swung round. "Remember that bitch at school? Remember her? She got upset because I slapped your face. Like this." He struck Curle across the cheek, and stood for a moment before showing his teeth in a parody of a smile. "Nothing ever changes," he said.

When Jill the neighbour appeared, Curle was sitting on the bench under the tree.

"I hope you didn't mind me interfering."

He looked up at her dully. With an effort, he said, "Not as bad as it sounded."

"Whoever he was, he sounded like a madman." A ruddy-cheeked widow, full of surplus energy and missing the intrigues of the boarding house she'd once run, curiosity made her more animated than he'd ever seen her. "Just as well I was cleaning out the shed."

"Just a misunderstanding. He apologised and left."

"Did he say something about his wife?"

"No. Why would he do that? He was — a writer — I did a review — and he took exception to it. As I said, all sound and fury."

"Ah . . ." Something in her tone told him that she had him down now as an adulterer. Before he could try again, she exclaimed, "Oh dear, did you knock them over?"

Following her gaze, he saw that the holder was lying on its side and that spilled peanuts were piled under the bench.

"Let me help you to gather them up."

"No!" he said more sharply than he'd intended. "No . . . Really, I'll manage."

He waited her out, but even after she'd gone he sat motionless staring at the nuts scattered on the grass, his hands trembling too badly for him to attempt to pick them up.

CHAPTER
FORTY-TWO

I've fallen in love with my wife and had my face slapped, Curle thought, and it's not twelve o'clock yet.

He got up slowly from the garden bench. Going back into the house, his legs felt stiff as if he'd aged thirty years. Behind him, the nuts still lay where they'd fallen, but he didn't care. It was good to feel irresponsible. Let the rats eat them.

The need to get away from his own thoughts drove him out of the house. It was one of those days when the cloud cover shone with a cold pearly glow. The air stung his cheeks as he walked down to the bus stop. After a bit, he began to move more briskly, swinging his arms, with the air of a man in charge of his life.

At the end of his journey, the same deceptive energy took him up the stairs to Jonah's office at a run. The personal assistant, Alice, was at her desk, her door open.

Panting after the effort, he said, "I'm getting too old for that stuff."

"Walking up stairs?"

"Running!" he protested. And added as his breathing eased, "I wouldn't mind a word, but if he's busy it doesn't matter."

"He's gone for lunch."

"Already?"

She flipped open a desk calendar. "He'd an appointment at twelve, but he cancelled it when Mr Todd phoned."

"Brian Todd?"

She smiled. "You know him? He came in last week. He's a charmer, isn't he?"

Curle managed a smile. "For you, maybe."

"I think most women would think that way."

It had never struck him before that she might be stupid.

"So they're having lunch?"

"At the Centotre. You know, in George Street?"

He walked up to St Andrews Square and along George Street. He'd heard of the Centotre, a new Italian café-bar and restaurant, but hadn't been there and, having chosen the wrong pavement, almost missed the entry, muted on the façade of a fine Georgian building. Having come that far, pacing along like a man late for an appointment, his steps faltered to a halt. Stopping was a mistake. Better to have gone with his body's momentum and let it march him up the steps. What can he do to me in a public place? he thought. And then, If he so much as looks at me the wrong way, I'll stab him in the eye with a fork. And gathering his self-respect, he went inside.

The agent looked up in surprise at his approach. He was alone at the table.

Curle rested his hand on the back of a chair.

"Alice told me you were having lunch with Todd."

"Did she, indeed? I'll have to smack her wrist. Not that it isn't always a pleasure to see you."

"She must have thought Todd was pleasure as well. Not business, I mean."

Jonah frowned.

"Why don't you sit down?" he said. "Join us for lunch."

"Why not?"

They drank a glass of wine and twenty minutes passed. Fidgeting with his napkin, Jonah suggested that they should order. Curle, whose mind wasn't on food, followed his choices so that they both had chicken broth and broiled fish.

"You're being very quiet," Jonah said as they pushed their plates away.

Curle looked around. The group around the nearest table was getting up to go.

"I was waiting for Todd to come."

"Coffee?" Jonah signalled to the waiter. "I doubt if he'll be coming now."

"I did want to talk to you." Curle tried for a smile and felt it quiver and fade.

"Is something wrong?"

"I have to talk to someone." He fell silent as the plates were cleared away.

Jonah looked at his watch. "Half an hour enough? I've got a pile of stuff back at the office."

"It's not easy."

"*In media res*," Jonah said. "Jump right in. Good rule, if you want to tell a story."

Curle had wanted to talk about Todd. He'd intended to tell how he had come to his house that morning. Not smooth, not smiling, not the man they'd been meeting after a lapse of so many years. How had his neighbour described it? Like a madman. But as he braced himself to start, he realised that there was no way in the world he could confess to this old friend that it had happened again. For the second time in his life, Todd had slapped his face. For the second time, he had taken it and done nothing. The crucial difference being that this time he had done nothing not as a boy, but a man.

"Well?" Jonah smiled and raised an eyebrow.

"The night before last —" he began.

"I know!" Jonah exclaimed. "I saw it in the papers!"

"What?"

"That woman being killed in the flat under Ali Fleming's. Such a grotesque coincidence."

Curle made a gesture as if sweeping something aside.

"The night before last, Liz didn't come home," he heard himself saying.

He told the story from when he had sat in his car waiting to follow her, through the journey to the hotel, seeing the two of them in the bar, taking a room, wakening in the morning, finding her car gone. Jonah listened attentively, interjecting a question or comment at intervals. "You watched her car?" in a tone of mild outrage. "Brian? Brian was with her?" sounding shocked. "You just sat in the room all night?"

"No, I got into bed and slept for some of it," Curle said sullenly. Telling the story didn't make him feel good about himself, he regretted having started it.

When he'd finished, Jonah said censoriously, "I have to say you deserved all you got."

"I'm not the bloody adulterer!"

"Best not to know," Jonah said. "Wouldn't you be happier if you didn't know that Brian had fucked your wife?"

"He didn't!"

"Didn't?"

And Curle repeated what Liz had told him about Todd laughing at her and leaving.

"Not an adulterer then," Jonah observed. He broke into a smile. "That's an enormous relief. Must be. For you, I mean."

"Just a bastard! I don't think he's sane." And he thought again of how Todd had looked as he burst into the garden that morning; and again couldn't bear to speak of it.

"Oh, I don't think it's a mad thing to do. You wouldn't have to be insane, just very very malicious. Appallingly malicious, in fact. It's very troubling." Smile gone as quickly as it had come, he chewed on his knuckles and thought for a moment. "The thing is, he must hate you. I can't think why. After all this time, it's very strange. I believe we must make an effort to find the reason."

As soon as the word had been used, Curle understood that, yes, it must be that he was hated. Hatred, he had felt it not as an abstraction, but palpable as flesh meeting flesh. Now it was all around, a mist darkening the air, a foul taste in the mouth. It changed the world and made it unbearable. In the end, the rats got everything.

In the end, the rats got everything.

He must have said it aloud.

"Don't start thinking like that, for God's sake. That kind of talk is bollocks," Jonah responded. "Great swollen sodding writers' bollocks."

With an exclamation, he looked at his watch. The half-hour he'd offered had stretched to more than twice that length.

"Oh dear, another appointment missed. And I'm due to meet someone in the next ten minutes." Catching the eye of a waiter, he scribbled on the air in the universal sign of wanting a bill. "I really am sorry. We could meet later?"

"No," Curle said. "I have to get back anyway. Kerr will be home from school."

"Tomorrow then, if you want. Ring me. I'll make time."

They walked back to Jonah's office in silence, each lost in his own thoughts.

As they parted at the street entrance, Jonah asked, "Are you sure you're all right?"

"I'll manage," Curle said.

Time to go back and wait for his son to come home.

CHAPTER
FORTY-THREE

The following morning, Curle announced that he would take Kerr to school. A subdued and withdrawn Liz made no objection. Since she needed the car for work, however, and the Vectra, which he'd been driving without a spare, had picked up a flat tyre, they would have to walk.

"It's raining," Kerr announced.

Curle checked out of the window.

"Drizzling," he said firmly.

"You don't need to come. I can go by myself."

"I'll enjoy the walk. Get your coat on. We don't want to be late."

Curle followed him into the hall. It looked wet rather than cold outside, so he put on an old blue anorak he kept in the cupboard under the stairs. He waited at the door until Kerr trudged back down from his bedroom.

"Got everything?"

"Other people go to school by themselves. Graeme goes by himself."

"His mother fetches you both home."

"In the morning. He goes by himself in the morning."

"I don't think so."

"Sometimes. He does sometimes. Why can't I? I'm not a baby."

"Of course, you're not. Do it for your mother's sake. You know she worries."

It was the easy way out. You're a manly little chap. I'm a man. Man to man, blame it on the woman. A good preparation for life. Only this time, Curle was stabbed by a horrible sense of guilt. It took only a second to place the cause. He was betraying his wife. Again. What the hell had he been thinking of when he'd told Jonah about Liz going to the hotel and being humiliated by Brian Todd? What kind of man would do a thing like that? He remembered his father once telling him that his own mother had come to see him as a baby. She'd bent over the crib and said after inspecting him, "Ah, weel, ye'll never mak a gentleman o that yin." She'd died when he was seventeen. He'd a memory of wrinkles, fierce blue eyes, jet-black hair. Black hair? She must have been over ninety. Old witch!

As they went down the path, he said awkwardly, "We both worry. I know you're not a baby. Put up with us. Wait till the summer. When you start school again in August, you can walk by yourself. I'll speak to your mother about it."

They walked along in silence. The fine rain washed the cold air. The world smelled as if it had been freshly laundered. He took the school bag from the boy and carried it dangling from his hand.

At the school gates, Kerr took the bag back and stood hesitating. At last, he asked, "Promise?"

Fortunately, Curle understood at once. He nodded firmly. "I'll speak to her."

He stood by the railings as mothers came and went. Cars drew up and disgorged uniformed muppets. Once through the circling eddies of children he spotted Kerr alone by the wall. He could imagine the boy's embarrassment at having a father who remained fixed in place, one hand gripping a railing, instead of marching off to work: *places to go people to see.* Mercifully, the bell rang at last, though even then he stood and watched until the last child from the last column had been sucked in through the entrance.

What was the point of going home? His deadline was in ruins. The last timetable he'd drawn up just before Ali's death had estimated he'd have to write three thousand words a day to meet it, every day, no weekend breaks, no flu, no depression lay-offs, every day without exception until the day it was due to be posted. On good form he could manage five hundred a day. He wasn't going to make it. Being a murder suspect, wasn't that an excuse? Maybe not for a crime writer.

He spent the morning in the Central Library. Wandering up and down the open shelves, he picked at random a book on Wagner, one of Agnes Mure Mackenzie's histories of Scotland and a biography of an Indian astrophysicist who discovered black holes and was humiliated for his efforts by Sir Arthur Stanley Eddington, who'd posed as his friend. He read them turn and turn about, a chapter here and another there, until they fused into a broth in his head and the morning was disposed of. As he came out blinking into daylight and set off to walk down the Mound to Princes Street, he consoled himself with the thought he could call it research. At once a lively sense of guilt conjured up a sceptical tax inspector: "And have you actually started this novel about a big contralto in a kilt who goes through a black hole to the next universe in pursuit of this wee Indian bloke she fancies to tell him he's won a Nobel Prize?" "Might have."

On Princes Street, he lingered at shop windows, staring at shoe displays as if deep in thought. As he tried to hold off images of murder and arrest, random thoughts scurried around like mice trying to escape a cat and he realised how tired he had grown of his own company. At a brisk pace, he set off going west towards Jonah's office. Once there, he baulked at going in, shamed by the idea he might start talking again about Liz. If he's in a meeting, what excuse could I possibly make for barging in? I should have phoned, he told himself. He might be with anyone, somebody I know, Edinburgh was a small world. After what had been in the papers, he wanted to avoid people he knew. Tainted by suspicion, he felt like a man with a sickness. Unclean, unclean. He walked on, slowly this time, drifting. The garden in the middle of Charlotte Square was like a vacant room waiting to be filled by the bustle of the Book Festival in August. Staring through the railings at the forlorn grass, he remembered how lonely Kerr had looked standing against the wall of the crowded playground. In George Street, scanning the faces of passers-by (they couldn't all be without a care in the world — that wouldn't make sense), he realised he'd washed ashore outside the Italian place where Jonah and he had eaten the day before. There was no reason to believe he'd be taking lunch there two days running. On the other hand, there was no harm in trying.

In the restaurant, there was no sign of Jonah. No surprise there. What he hadn't expected was to look down and find himself standing over ACC Bob Fairbairn alone at a table. Perversely, it was the look of alarm that brought him to a stop.

"Bob! Good to see you. It's been a while."

He listened to himself being hearty, false as a six-pound note.

To his surprise, Fairbairn, too habitually the diplomat for snubbing to come easily to him, made an attempt at a smile. His eyes, however, ran over Curle head to foot and came to a verdict.

Registering this, Curle had to stop himself from rubbing his chin. He'd made only a token gesture of shaving that morning since he was only walking down to the school. For the same reason, he'd shoved on the old anorak he wore for taking rubbish to the dump. Christ, he thought. Buddy can you spare a dime?

With a nod, he turned to make his escape only to find Fairbairn's lunch companion bearing down on him.

Joe Tilman came to an abrupt halt, glancing from Curle to his brother-in-law. He gave off the impression of an enormous contained energy, an arrested stillness like a jungle cat that could kill with a swipe of its paw.

Instead of swiping, though, the hand he lifted brushed slowly over the mane of iron-grey hair.

"You went to see my wife," he said quietly. "Do you know what you've done?"

I've been slapped, Curle thought. Once is enough.

Before he could say anything, Tilman went on, "She's in a mental home. The state she was in when I got home, you left me no choice. I've had her sectioned."

Curle was making his way blindly towards the vestibule, when he felt a tap on his shoulder. He turned, expecting Tilman.

"DI Meldrum is looking for you," Fairbairn told him. "It would be better if you went in yourself rather than waiting to be taken in. Shall I phone and tell him you're on your way?"

CHAPTER
FORTY-FOUR

In the days before the nightmare began, he had been shown around this building by the Assistant Chief Constable himself and been privately amused by the appetite of people in every profession to have their realities validated by fiction. He might even have been shown this room. He sat alone, having turned down the idea of a lawyer, facing Meldrum and McGuigan on the other side of a narrow table. After it had been switched on, he imagined he could hear a noise from the recording machine in moments of silence.

"I'm disappointed in you," Meldrum said. "What made you imagine you could get away with lying about being home the night Eva Johanson was killed?"

That was the beginning of a long strange day.

As happened before, he found himself confessing at least part of the truth with hardly even a token show of resistance. He was a talented fabulist, not a practised liar. At lying, any streetwise nine-year-old villain would have handled the detectives more brazenly. Timid and instinctively law-abiding, he admitted more or less at once to having spent the night in a hotel.

"You were meeting someone?" Meldrum asked.

"No!" His indignation was absurd, but genuine. "I needed time alone to think. That was all. Kerr, my son, was having a sleepover with friends and, I thought, I'll have a night away too. It was just an impulse."

"You take an overnight away from home often?" McGuigan asked.

"Not often. Occasionally at conferences or whatever."

"What about with Ali Fleming? All those years when she was your mistress. You never spent the night with Ali Fleming?"

Curle shook his head. It was true. McGuigan stared at him sceptically. Hard blue eyes in a tough handsome Scots Irish face; if he had a mistress as well as a wife, Curle thought, he'd have managed a weekend now and then, maybe even a holiday together, because he'd want it all, because he was braver, because he was less cautious. And he'd have had it all, until something happened and everything went smash. He was that type, too, one of the ones who self-destruct.

"Did you tell your wife you were going to be away?" Meldrum wondered.

Curle couldn't find a glib answer to that. He said hesitantly, "I left her a note."

"Why would she say you were there all night?"

"She thought she was helping me."

"You let her do that?" McGuigan wondered. "You know a lie like that could get her into trouble?"

"Wives can't be forced to give evidence against their husbands."

"Not the same."

Before Curle could answer, Meldrum asked, "How would she be helping you? What did she think you'd done?"

He found that although his absurd uncontrollable imagination conjured up only too easily unwanted pulp fiction associations for McGuigan of back rooms, bright lights, even rubber hoses, he was more wary of the big dour man with the workman's hands.

"Nothing. I said I'd spent the night at home, so she supported me. And you took it for granted she'd been home."

Meldrum nodded at some thought of his own. "And wasn't she?"

Alarmed, Curle blurted, "I didn't mean — I didn't say she wasn't. All I meant was all she had to do was agree. She wasn't really lying, she was just agreeing."

McGuigan opened his mouth to snarl, Curle thought, at the nonsense he was talking, but Meldrum sighed and said, "Let's go and talk to the people at the hotel."

He sat in the back of the unmarked police car, watching the innocent pavements go by as the streets unwound at high speed. McGuigan, it seemed, was no respecter of limits. The sky, grey when they got into the car, had cleared as they pulled into a parking space outside the Smiddy Hotel. Stepping out into the brightness, feeling the warmth of the sun on his shoulders, Curle thought how good it would be on a day like this to go walking with Kerr on the paths between the open parks of the zoo.

The girl at the reception desk said she would fetch the manager. Curle recognised the hard-faced woman in her fifties who came out from a door at the rear, and from the way her gaze lingered on him he was sure the recognition was mutual. She offered the tall policeman a wary smile and took them back into the little room, cramped by a desk and filing cabinets, which she described as her office.

"Have you ever seen this man before?"

To Curle's relief, she nodded.

"Could you tell me when that was?" Meldrum asked.

"Day before yesterday. Later on. In the evening. He took a room. It's in the register."

"Could we see it?"

She got up reluctantly. When she came back with the book, she laid it on the desk, sat down and opened it.

"Just show us the entry," McGuigan said.

She turned the book and pushed it across to him.

"Four down."

"Sure?"

"I've a good memory."

"Fine." He grinned. "So I don't need to check the other pages?"

She stared at him sourly.

He pushed the register to Meldrum, putting his finger on the entry, tapping it on the page once and then again.

"He signed in just after seven o'clock," she said.

"And he was alone?" Meldrum asked.

"That's what it says." Meldrum stared at her. After a moment of the silent treatment, she added, "He asked where the restaurant was."

"So?"

"He was looking for some couple that had been in the bar."

They talk about me as if I'm not here, Curle thought, staring at his hands as if pretending that he wasn't.

"Did he find them?"

"No idea."

"Really?"

". . . I don't think so. That's when he came back and asked for a room."

"Can you describe this couple?"

"No."

"How did he know they'd been in the bar?"

"He looked."

"You like to explain that?"

Her heavy bosom rose and fell in a sigh at the unreasonableness of the question. "I was at the desk. He came in out of the rain, trailed water all over the floor, looked in the bar and went out again. Came back later, looked in the bar again, then asked where the restaurant was."

"And you can't describe this couple?"

"Never saw them."

"Busy night, was it?"

"What do you mean?"

"If we checked the bar takings, restaurant takings, lot of people in?"

She shrugged. "It was quiet. We're always quiet except at the weekends. But I don't stand at the desk all night. I've got things to do. So whoever they were," she glanced at Curle, "I missed them, all right?"

226

"So Mr Curle here checked in around seven. When did he leave?"

"He paid for his room in the morning." For the first time, she volunteered a statement unprompted: "Just don't ask me if he was in his room all night. Like I say, there are things I might miss."

Back in the car, McGuigan said, "That was like pulling teeth."

He hadn't switched on and both men turned to look at Curle in the back seat.

Meldrum said, "Want to tell us now?"

After a moment, McGuigan said, "Just above your name, there's a Mr and Mrs John Smith booked in. For a double room. That sound like an old joke to you?"

"We can guess who the woman was," Meldrum said. "Who was the man?"

"We can always ask your wife," McGuigan said.

How could it be another betrayal when he had been driven into a corner? He admitted that he had been following his wife, and that the man was Brian Todd. A little smirk tugged at the corners of McGuigan's lips.

Meldrum, however, expressionless as ever, asked sharply, "Todd? The man in the pub the night Ali Fleming was killed? The one you were at school with? I thought the two of you had lost touch?"

"We had."

"So where did your wife meet him?"

"He came to the house."

"When would that be?"

"Just after Ali was murdered."

227

This time McGuigan smiled openly, a big wolfish grin showing a line of straight white teeth.

"As quick as that," he said.

Angered, Curle said, "Nothing happened!"

"You're sure of that?"

"I trust my wife!"

With a sinking heart, he could see the smirk on McGuigan's face as he asked, why was he following her then?

It was Meldrum, however, who put the next question.

"When did she tell you nothing happened? Did you go to their double room at the hotel?"

Miserably, Curle shook his head. "I didn't know which room it was. She told me next day at home."

"So she stayed the night?"

"Yes. But not with Todd. He left — he left after she told him it wasn't on."

Meldrum nodded. It seemed the question of whether or not Liz had been truthful didn't interest him. Instead he said, "You can prove where you were at seven o'clock that night and where you were the next morning. It's the bit in between that's the problem."

"I didn't kill Eva Johanson. For God's sake, what reason would I have had to kill her?"

"What reason would anybody have had?" McGuigan asked. "On the other hand, we're pretty sure the same man murdered her and Ali Fleming. And we know you had a reason to kill Ali Fleming."

"That place leaks like a sieve," Meldrum said, nodding at the hotel. "You could have slipped out and come back."

"I didn't."

"All we know is you were alone in the room," Meldrum said.

They studied Curle for a moment, and then satisfied, as if by an unspoken agreement both turned to face forward. McGuigan turned on the engine.

"No," Curle said.

"What?"

"I wasn't alone."

He eased up and reached for the billfold in his hip pocket. Meldrum who'd turned back watched as he took a folded slip of paper from the front compartment.

"The number's written on it," he said, passing it over.

CHAPTER
FORTY-FIVE

They picked him up at the corner of Leith Walk and Macdonald Street, a bulky man in his forties wearing a faded leather jacket.

As he slid into the seat beside Curle, Meldrum passed the folded slip of paper back to him.

"We've tried a couple of times. She's been switched off."

"She'll still be in her bed," Leather Jacket said. "They're all lazy cows. Is this out of a Bible? Where did you get it?"

McGuigan said, "Mr Curle got it in the drawer beside his hotel bed the other night. Somebody had written the number in it, and he gave it a ring."

Curle stared straight ahead as, from the corner of his eye, he saw Leather Jacket squinting at him.

"How did you know what it was?" he asked.

Curle ignored the question.

"Mobile phone number? In a hotel drawer? Might have been a plumber, but he didn't need a plumber." McGuigan laughed. "Just shows, it pays to advertise."

"You shouldn't have torn the page out," Leather Jacket said, trying Curle again. "Not out of a Bible. That's bad luck."

"Not a lot," McGuigan said. "It was a Protestant Bible."

"Is there any other kind?" Leather Jacket asked. "Take the next on the left. I'll bring her down."

"You have a key?" McGuigan asked.

"No. I don't have a fucking key. Hey, stop the car!"

McGuigan hauled the car to a stop at the edge of the pavement. It was as if he'd conjured a parking space out of thin air.

Leather Jacket opened his door and shouted, "Magda!" then cursed and clambered out of the car.

They watched him as he walked back along the pavement. Just before the corner he turned in under the mortar and pestle sign of a chemist's. When he came out, he was with a young woman. Her blonde hair was cut close around a narrow skull. It was hard to tell what it was that marked her out. The skirt was very short, but lots of women wore them that way. Maybe it was something about the way she slouched to a stop, hip shot, by the car. Whatever it was, there wasn't any doubt she was for sale.

Bending to the window Meldrum had wound down, he said, "She'll have to do her shopping later."

Meldrum said something too quietly for Curle to catch.

Leather Jacket opened the car door and held the girl's head down as she got in.

Through the side window, Curle watched him walking away. He caught the warm staleness of powdered skin from the girl and, faint enough to be his imagination, what might have been the lingering smell of sex.

"I not do anything," she said. She glanced sideways at Curle without moving her head. "What he say I do? I don't steal. Don't do anything wrong."

Meldrum was twisted half round, one hand resting on the back of the seat. He flicked a finger to indicate Curle. "You know this man?"

"I never see him in my whole life."

"She's the one!" Curle exclaimed.

Ignoring him, she said to Meldrum, "That is fucking truth."

"Aye, right," Meldrum said. He faced front again, massaging his neck with one hand. "Back to the hotel, we'll sort it out there."

McGuigan switched on and steered out into the traffic.

It was an uncomfortable journey. The girl Magda kept her attention determinedly turned to the window. She hadn't tried to resist being put into the car; she'd made no protest at being taken off to the hotel. In her own country and since, no doubt, she had been obedient to uniformed police, pliant before bureaucrats, cowed by pimps and violent strangers. Her passivity gave Curle a sense of a life lived without even the illusion of autonomy. It was that memory of her vulnerability which had made him ashamed when he woke alone in the hotel room. He had torn the page with the number on it out of the Gideon Bible and hidden it in his wallet to prevent her being exploited by men like him: an explanation he would keep to himself

232

for fear of being mocked. Absurd, self-serving, hypocritical, like so much of his moral life the impulse was contradictory but not entirely contemptible.

CHAPTER
FORTY-SIX

Jonah Murray wasn't a man who entertained at home. There were bachelors who went in for cooking gourmet meals, blocks bristling with best-quality kitchen knives, heavy-bottomed copper French pans, splash-proof aprons with masculine motifs. He wasn't one of them. His natural habitat was the restaurant, found by himself rather than too fashionable, for leisurely working lunches and the occasional dinner for half a dozen close friends. It fitted with his oxymoronic emotional strategy of embracing people while holding them at arms' length. That Curle was surprised, as he set out for Jonah's flat, to realise he'd never actually been inside it, was testimony to how effectively the strategy worked.

He drove into the Queen's Park at the Palace of Holyrood and turned right up the winding road and then down sharply past the loch. In Duddingston he made a mistake and had to do a three-point turn in a narrow road before finding at last the converted townhouse where Jonah lived in the penthouse apartment.

He pressed the entrance buzzer and heard the security door unlock before he could speak.

Coming out of the lift into a narrow hallway, he was lifting his hand to knock with the little brass gargoyle head when Jonah opened the door. At sight of Curle, his face went slack with astonishment.

"Barclay!"

"You were expecting someone else?"

"I've a table booked for dinner."

"This will only take a minute," Curle promised grimly.

Given no choice, reluctantly Jonah led the way inside. He stood in the middle of the floor and didn't invite Curle to sit down.

"You said a minute. I really have to be going almost at once."

At any other time, Curle would have been avid for detail of the way Jonah lived. As it was, even in his state of contained anger, he couldn't help noticing the baby grand that sat in one corner. He hadn't known that Jonah played the piano, or even that he was interested in music. A man who managed his life in compartments: music for those who were interested (Curle wasn't), books for others, and paintings too, presumably, since the walls were crowded with pictures.

"I've been with the police all afternoon," Curle said.

He scanned Jonah's face for a sign of guilt.

"May one ask why?"

"They found out I lied about being at home the night that woman was murdered."

"The one in the flat under Ali?" All that Curle saw was what he had seen so often on his friend's face: the eagerness of the born gossip.

"And that meant Liz was lying to them as well. They didn't like being lied to."

"But you didn't know this woman. What could her murder have to do with you?"

"You're the only one who could have told them. I can't make sense of that. Why would you do that?"

Jonah flushed with indignation. "I didn't tell them! I'm insulted that you should think so!" But his gaze, which had been fixed on Curle, slid furtively away.

"What is it?"

"Nothing."

"You do understand I might have been arrested for murder?"

"But you weren't!"

"Because I phoned for a whore."

"What are you talking about?"

"To come to the hotel." He was shaken by a spasm of self-disgust. "Pretty, isn't it? While I thought my wife was committing adultery along the corridor, I was spanking and fucking a whore."

"Don't tell me this. I don't want to listen."

As they stood silently confronting one another, poised for the next challenge, an echoing insistent banging sounded on the outer door.

"Oh, dear," Jonah said.

Curle waited, listening with an uneasy presentiment.

"How did you get up here?" he heard Jonah asking from the hall.

"Are you going to move your arse?" Did he know that voice? "Somebody hadn't closed the security door properly."

"I've complained about that repeatedly," Jonah was saying over his shoulder as he returned.

Brian Todd followed him into the room.

"What's this?" He spoke to Jonah not Curle. "What the hell do you think you're doing?"

Curle had seen Jonah in many moods, but never so defensive, never so flustered, never cowed.

"Barclay came about that poor woman who was killed. The police wanted to talk to him about her."

Todd shifted his gaze to Curle.

"You know how she died?" he asked. Expecting any question but that, Curle gaped at him.

"Are you talking about the woman?" Jonah asked. Bewilderment didn't suit him. It furrowed his face with lines like the marks of ageing.

"The woman," Todd repeated, mimicking the tone in mockery. "She was strangled to death. Her windpipe was crushed. And after she was dead, this time it was after, she was beaten to a pulp. Eva Johanson was her name. The woman."

He moved his shoulders, shrugging like a boxer in the ring. He gave off energy like heat, a body packed with muscles.

"Was that — that wasn't in the papers," Jonah said.

"A client told me."

Curle remembered the talk of a reporter whom Todd had helped with his tax problems. He'd taken the man's existence for granted. Suddenly he didn't believe in him. But if the reporter didn't exist, how could Todd know how the women had been killed? Was he making it up? What kind of sick pleasure could there be in that?

Todd had answered Jonah's question casually without looking at him, never taking his eyes from Curle. Now he said, "I didn't expect to see you again."

Casual, again. It was the only word. It was the assumption of power over him in Todd's tone, casual, unquestioned, that transformed Curle's feelings. Before that moment, he had disliked Todd, been scarred by the memory of him, had even at one time been obsessed by him. Afterwards, like the tempering of a beaten sword plunged into icy water, he hated him. He had no words for it, though. If he'd had a weapon, he would have attacked him.

As Curle stood silent, Todd disconcerted him by smiling. A grimace that bared his upper teeth, there was no humour in it. "I thought you'd be in a cell. You're a cat with nine lives." He put his arm around Jonah's shoulder and asked, "What's it going to take?" He squeezed the smaller man tightly to him, knuckles whitening with the force of his grip. "That'll give us something to talk about." He laughed at the expression on Curle's face. "Pillow talk."

The stricken look on Jonah's face as he hung like a doll in that awful grip was beyond bearing.

As Curle made blindly for the door, he heard Todd's voice, asking in mock surprise, "How long have you two been friends? I knew as soon as I looked at him."

On the way down in the lift, he began to retch. Hard dry shudders shook him so that it would have been a relief to vomit. He hadn't eaten since breakfast, however, so there was nothing to sick up.

238

CHAPTER
FORTY-SEVEN

At some point, he'd told Jonah that he was sure Bobbie Haskell was gay. Not like you and me, eh, buddy? I envy you your novelist's insight, Jonah had said. Was that satirical? What else could it be? In the past, Jonah had stroked Curle's ego by pointing out reviews blethering of his profound insight into human nature. The truth is, Curle thought, I know nothing.

Unable to cope with his own company, he lunched at the Arts Club to find the conversation dominated by a visiting American with a face like a Fox newscaster. One of those McCarthy types, he decided as he chewed without appetite, who carry all before them until they're caught with a hand in the till or up a choirboy's cassock. As penance for his sins of incomprehension, he listened without interruption as the guest's talk ranged from the current thirst for God to the need to get back in touch with nature. From the illustrations offered, he seemed to have derived his knowledge of mysticism and the mores of Scottish rural life from *The Da Vinci Code.*

He sat for a while after lunch; jerked awake on the realisation he'd dozed off; came out blinking into the light of a pale afternoon sun. He sauntered along

Princes Street from one store to another, wandering at last into Jenners and letting himself drift aimlessly with the crowd up through its maze of floors. Three Muslim women covered from head to toe as they bent over a display of fine porcelain caught his attention for a moment. Idly, he wondered if human nature could be so easily muffled. Did one woman in a burqua ever turn to another to ask, Do my eyes look big in this? He drank coffee and ate a cake in the café, sitting at a table alone. He would have liked to go home and spend time with Kerr. The boy would be back from school by this time, but he'd be cared for since it was one of Liz's afternoons off. It was all too complicated. He looked at his watch. Not home; he had somewhere else to go, but it was still too early. He set himself to passing the rest of the afternoon.

At six, he was in George Street and began to walk west, still not hurrying, wanting to give Bobbie Haskell time to get home from work. It gave him time, too, to plan his approach. He didn't have any hope of success.

At Royal Circus, there was no answer when he pressed Haskell's buzzer. He tried three times then gave up, crossed the road and went along Great King Street, cut up Dundas Street and made his way back again. This time a voice asked, "Yes?" He leaned close to the grille and gave his name. At once, the lock was released.

On the top floor, Haskell waited in his doorway. He was wearing chinos and a shirt open at the neck. Just back from work presumably, he'd replaced outdoor shoes with a pair of light moccasin-style slippers.

"Don't tell me," he said pleasantly. "The shortbread was so delicious, you've come back for more."

Curle was basically a diffident man but, without wishing to, there were people to whom he knew himself to be superior. He had that feeling about Haskell, and as a result felt more comfortable with him than he usually did with acquaintances.

"Your downstairs lock was working this time," he said.

Stepping back to let him enter, Haskell looked puzzled. "It usually does."

"Not always though?"

"You have to be careful how you shut it."

They were standing in the hall. As Haskell closed the door, Curle made as if to go into the front room where Linda Fleming and he had been entertained. With a light touch on his arm, Haskell turned him the other way.

"I want you to see this."

An open door gave a glimpse of the kitchen, a pine table, a rack of cooking implements on the wall by a double oven, a work surface with a block of knives and a wooden bowl standing beside a board with a half-chopped salad. Since the flat shared its layout with the one below, Curle knew that the room opposite into which he was being led must be Haskell's bedroom.

"You must have wondered where they all were," Haskell said.

Time slipped and as he stepped inside, it was as if he was going into Ali's bedroom. She would be standing by the bed, lying on it, laughing afterwards, her face close to his.

It was a square room, not particularly well lit, since the windows at the back were tall and narrow rather than the ample bow windows on the front of the building. Three bookcases, each tall enough to reach the high ceiling, dwarfed the single bed placed under the window.

"I keep them all in here."

"Books?" Curle guessed.

"What else?" A small frown creased the fine skin between Haskell's pale eyebrows. He stared at Curle as if wondering whether he had intended a joke. If so, clearly he was not amused. "It's a thing of mine. I won't have them shelved anywhere else in the flat. But they're here all right. I didn't want you to think I was some kind of philistine. So many houses now and there's never a book in sight. Television and record players and a mini bar in the corner, isn't that right? As a writer, it must make you wonder what the world has come to."

"You have a lot of books," Curle said carefully. It had the merit of being true. Feeling something else was required, he added, "Beautiful bookcases."

"They belonged to an uncle of mine. He left me them in his will. Too tall for a modern flat. I had to keep them in store until my aunt died." Puzzled for an instant, Curle recalled being told at some point that the flat had been bought with an inheritance from an aunt. "Aren't I lucky? You could say I've everything I want."

Curle found this too effusive to answer. He kept silence until they were in the front room. Seated, he glanced round and, for something to say, remarked, "Plenty of space for a bookcase. One of them would look well in here."

This was a mistake, however, for Haskell looked offended. Putting back a lock of blond hair, he said, "I thought I'd made it clear. I don't keep books in here. I'm quite particular about that."

Who was it? Curle wondered. George Douglas Brown? Who'd made the point that stupid people would seize on some arbitrary habit and follow it inflexibly as a mark of individuality.

Haskell, however, had an explanation. "For me books should be private. If you took me into a stranger's house and showed me his books, you'd be surprised how much I could tell about him. Or her."

"Or her," Curle noted.

"Yes. Do you want something to drink?"

"No, thanks. I don't want to keep you from your meal."

"Oh, it won't take long tonight. Just a simple salad with a bottle of white wine. I was opening it when the buzzer went. You're sure you wouldn't take a glass?"

"Absolutely!" Curle said a shade too emphatically.

"Oh, well."

After an awkward silence, Curle said, "Can I ask you something about the night Ali was killed?"

Haskell stiffened. "If I killed her? Is that what you want to know?"

"No, of course not."

"That awful bloody woman downstairs thinks I did. Do you know that?"

"I'd no idea. I mean, you must be mistaken."

"When you came here for afternoon tea, she stole something. She claimed she wanted a pee and took her chance to wander about the place. I only realised once you'd gone."

"I find that hard to believe," Curle said.

"Believe it!"

Curle thought quickly, trying to work out how to use this unexpected turn in the conversation to his advantage. "If it is the case," he said, "she's just threshing about because she's distraught over her sister's death. She desperately needs to know who killed her. You can see how natural that is."

"I can't bring Ali back."

"None of us can." Curle felt the sting of unwanted tears. "But it would help, it would help me too, if whoever killed her was punished."

"It wasn't me."

"I know that."

"You're sure?" To Curle's eye, there was something pathetic in the blond man's plea for reassurance.

"The night Ali was killed Jonah Murray and I left you in the pub with Brian Todd. You remember?"

Stupid question.

"I'll never forget that night," Haskell said.

"Did you tell him about Ali and me?"

"What was there to tell?"

"Don't play silly games. You knew we were lovers. Did you tell Todd?"

244

". . . I was drunk. I'm not really a drinker, apart from wine. After you two left, he bought whiskies. I didn't want it, but he insisted."

"So you told him?"

"I think so."

"What does that mean?"

"I told you, I'm not used to drinking so much. I may have done."

"How did that happen?"

"I think I told him that I lived in the flat above a friend of yours."

"A friend?"

"He kept on at me."

"And you told him I visited her."

"For years, I said." He stopped realising what he'd admitted. "I'm sorry."

It was more than Curle had expected to learn. The stirring of excitement, though, was dampened at once. There was a difficulty. "I don't suppose you told him where you lived?"

Haskell bit his lip, staring suddenly. "Wait a minute. What's this about?" His eyes narrowed. "Are you thinking this fellow Todd . . ." He baulked at putting the idea into words. "If that's what you're thinking, it doesn't make sense. He didn't know her. He'd never even heard of her until that night."

All of which was true, but he hadn't raised the obvious objection.

"But he did know where you lived? You told him where you lived?"

Curle held his breath.

"I had to. He gave me a lift home."

"You took him up to your flat?"

"No! Of course not."

"Did you watch him drive away?"

"No. I thanked him and he went off. I imagine that's what happened . . . What else would happen?"

"Is there any chance you didn't close the street door properly when you went in?"

Haskell threw up his hands. "I was drunk. I go in and out every day. I suppose I shut it."

"Did you tell the police about Todd running you home?"

"Yes — not that they were interested. I mean, why on earth would they be?"

They wouldn't be. But then, Curle thought, they don't know there's a history between Todd and me. What was it Jonah had said?: *He must hate you very much; we must find out why.*

CHAPTER
FORTY-EIGHT

Curle was on the second flight down when he heard the sound of Haskell's door being closed. He turned and, stepping softly, quickly remounted the stairs.

When Linda Fleming opened the door, he put his fingers to his lips and mouthed, "Can I come in?"

After a moment's hesitation, she stepped aside. He went in past her and without waiting for an invitation made his way to the front room and sat down.

When she'd joined him, he said, "I've just been with Haskell."

"Oh!" Her face lit up as she took her seat opposite him. "I see."

He said, "I wanted to put your mind at rest. I'm certain he isn't the one." There was no need to explain what he meant by that.

As the animation drained away, he was shocked to see how much she had aged since their last meeting. She hadn't brushed her hair and, without make-up, it straggled around a pale face marked by dark clown circles under the eyes.

She turned her head away from him. "I didn't sleep last night."

"You shouldn't stay here." He felt an impulse of genuine concern. "It's doing you harm."

"How can I leave?"

"What's to stop you? Get an agent to put the flat on the market and go home."

"You're not being honest!" she exclaimed.

"What?"

"I'm just asking you to be honest with me. Haven't I the right?"

"I'm sorry — I've no idea, what do you mean?"

"You ask me to give up. You're not giving up. Why else would you be seeing him?" She jerked a hand at the ceiling. "I don't need protecting. So don't lie to me about him. I know he killed my sister."

"But he's gay."

"What makes you think that?" Not waiting for an answer, she added scornfully, "Who else could it be, if it isn't him?"

She watched him with an expression of growing incredulity as he told her about Brian Todd.

When he'd finished, she shook her head and said slowly, "He killed Ali because he bullied you at school?"

He flushed. "He hates me for some reason."

"What has that to do with a woman he'd never seen or even heard of?"

"Because she was mine."

"That isn't a reason to kill someone."

"Maybe he didn't intend to kill her." No sooner had the thought come to him than it seemed enormously persuasive. "Maybe he went there to talk to her. Maybe he was arrogant enough to think she'd let him make

248

love to her. When she didn't, he tried to rape her and . . . it went wrong."

"Went wrong! You mean he beat her face, smashed all the bones in her face. And stamped on her. My sister, you're talking about my sister. Oh, Christ," Linda Fleming said, "you're all so sick." She moved both hands across her face, pressing it gently, as if feeling the bones. "Could you leave me alone now? Please."

He got to his feet.

At the door, he paused and said, "He knows his diary is missing."

"Are you sure?"

He was shamed by her fear.

Wanting to comfort her, he said, "It doesn't matter. There wasn't anything in it."

"But can he be sure of that?" she cried.

There was silence for a moment. Then in a different voice, she said again, "Can he be sure?"

Torn between wanting to get away and pity for her isolation and vulnerability, he offered her the number of his mobile phone and escaped.

CHAPTER
FORTY-NINE

Saturday morning, Curle ate the food Liz put in front of him without tasting it, trying to decide what to do. Constrained, Liz made no attempt to break into his silence. Since her meeting with Brian Todd at the hotel, since her passion of weeping over the death of Mae, a kind of embarrassment had kept husband and wife at arms' length. Crouched opposite Curle, his son ate without raising his head.

"I have to go out," Curle said, pushing his plate away.

They were the first words he had spoken.

Liz nodded. As soon as he stood, she reached over for his plate and cutlery, which she piled on her own ready to clear away.

The boy ate on, lifting the fork to his mouth, chewing and swallowing. Curle had been so absorbed he'd hardly been aware of the other two. Now he went round and laid his hand on Kerr's head.

"I won't be long," he said, and felt the little responsive movement under his hand.

All the way into the city, he seemed to feel it tingle on his palm.

He had no reason to believe that Meldrum would see him, always assuming he was there at all. Did policemen work on a Saturday? Of course, they did. Double time? Almost certainly not. The police had liaison officers who answered questions about police pay and conditions and other such trivia courteously and seriously. He'd used them himself.

As he was being led along the corridor to the office, he distracted himself with the thought of Meldrum's expression if he were to try a few such enquiries on him. I just called in, Inspector, to ask how many hours you work in an average week. At the first sight of the big man looking up from behind his desk, the distraction collapsed. Dry mouthed, Curle told himself he was innocent.

"Mr Curle," Meldrum said. He scratched what must have been a signature on a paper in front of him and laid his pen aside.

"It's good of you to see me."

"Oh, I'd be seeing you sooner or later."

It was said neutrally. There wasn't any kind of threat in it. It was no more than a matter of fact: however their business together was going to end had still to be settled.

Gestured to a seat, Curle found himself babbling as he sat down, "Saturday morning. Rotten time to be working."

The policeman looked at him quizzically. He's trying to decide, Curle thought, if I'm play-acting. Preparing a defence of idiocy.

"I should be with the others in the Incident Room," Meldrum said. "I had to take a meeting this morning, though." He glanced at his watch. "I was just leaving."

"I won't take up much of your time." He hesitated. He'd spent breakfast working out what he wanted to say, but now it wouldn't come to him. The man across the desk watched him in silence. Curle began again, "I'm concerned about Linda Fleming. I saw her yesterday."

Meldrum frowned. "Why?"

"She looks ill and stressed."

"I mean, why would you go to see her?"

Thrown out of his stride, Curle stared helplessly. "I'd just been to see Haskell." He chopped at the air. "This is a muddle. Can I explain it my own way?"

"It might be quicker."

Curle took the plunge. "I think I know who killed Ali," he said.

Meldrum took the news calmly. Leaning back, he said quietly, "Not the Classics Professor you told me about before, I hope. We've checked university departments from Aberdeen to Durham and points south. Put your mind at rest on that one."

"Not him. I'm sorry to have wasted your time."

"It didn't take long. But you have someone else now. You went to see Mr Haskell?"

"Not him either."

"You surprise me."

For the second time in two days, Curle explained his theory about Brian Todd. He'd spent the previous night awake going over it, and it was a better-honed version

252

than the one he'd offered Linda Fleming. He acknowledged, for example, how unlikely it was that a man would plan to murder a woman the moment after he'd learned of her existence. "But I don't think that's what he intended. He went to look at her. Probably he went to tell her what a weakling I was. I think then he tried to make love to her and it finished in rape. Once he'd done that, he had to kill her, and the way he did it — all that violence — that was the rage in him."

"Extraordinary," Meldrum said. "And you say he hates you?"

"Ask Jonah Murray. He believes the same thing. The three of us were at school together."

"My school wasn't such an exciting place."

"All right," Curle said, "it was a boarding school. Whatever you think of them, it does make a difference."

"From what I understand," Meldrum said, "they seem to be an important event in the lives of people like yourself."

"Yes."

"And yet am I not right in thinking that this man Todd hadn't seen you for thirty years?"

Curle nodded reluctantly. He could see where this was going.

"Is that not odd if he hated you as much as you say?"

But this was something Curle had thought about. "I don't think he hated me at school. He despised me. Maybe disliked me. But he does hate me now. Something happened in the years in between."

"Leave it with me." Meldrum looked at his watch again.

Taking the hint, Curle got to his feet.

"One thing more," he said. "About Linda Fleming."

Meldrum had got up and was walking him to the door. "Yes?"

"She's obsessed with the idea Haskell killed her sister. I know it's wrong."

"Did she tell you what she did with this diary she stole?"

"She's hidden it somewhere. The thing is, he knows she took it."

"How do you know that?"

"He told me. Dental appointments, stuff like that, how could it matter?"

Meldrum opened the door. It was a dismissal.

As Curle stepped into the corridor, he said, "Thank you for seeing me alone."

"I've got you on tape," Meldrum said. "Did I mention that?" Curle shook his head. A reflex brought the taste of vomit into the back of his mouth. "Well, you know now."

CHAPTER
FIFTY

Curle wasn't sure he wanted to speak to Jonah again. Indeed, he found it difficult to picture how they would ever manage to face one another. As with other, less extreme but similar, situations, his strategy had always been to do nothing for as long as humanly possible. It was the same principle as ignoring an in-tray; if you waited long enough, everything in it would have solved itself. Time was a great healer.

Two days wasn't long enough.

He'd come home from his interview with Meldrum to find a note propped against the milk jug on the kitchen table. Liz had taken Kerr into the shops and then over to Ster Century for lunch and most likely a film to go with it, if she could find one that was suitable. "I think he needs cheering up," she'd written.

When he read that, something like a stab of jealousy went through him. He knew his son probably loved his mother more than him. What little boy didn't love his mother best? But as little boys grew up, fathers got their chance. They taught their sons to play golf, bridge or poker, took them to football matches. How could mothers compete with that? A non-golfer, adulterer, murder suspect; had he blown his chance?

He was still chewing over that, together with a pilchard in tomato sauce balanced on a slice of wheaten bread, when Jonah phoned.

"I don't have the car," was Curle's excuse.

"You only have one car?"

"The Vectra needs a new tyre."

". . . I could come to you."

Waiting for him to arrive, Curle was filled with trepidation. What could he possibly want that would make him come all the way out here to the house? He had never visited Curle before, and there, however unworthy, was another cause for concern. It was a nice enough house, but nothing to boast about. In that it was like the old Vectra, both of them middle of the range, family models. Curle had been short of money for long enough to be canny about spending it even after he had some.

When Jonah arrived, however, he was a man on a mission, too intent to spare a glance for his surroundings. He sat down in the living room with his coat on and refused anything to drink.

Needing fortification, Curle opened the cabinet and poured himself a whisky.

As he sat down, Jonah leaned forward and asked, "Do you know what a phoenix company is?"

Curle stared in surprise. "Should I?"

"Didn't expect you to. You write murder stories. You don't have to know about anything to write murder stories."

Too uncomfortable to protest, Curle settled for a mouthful of whisky.

256

"A phoenix company is one that survives after it's been liquidated. Before it goes under, all its assets and cash have been handed over to a new firm which just happens to be owned by the same directors as the old one. They go on making money — only difference is that they've got rid of all their unpaid debts and taxes. You follow me?"

"Does that work?"

"Like the plague. It costs the country millions."

"It seems so obvious." Despite his confusion, Curle couldn't help absorbing information that might be useful at some point. "You'd think the police would crack down on it."

"That's where a good accountant comes in. A good crooked accountant. It wouldn't work without them. There aren't many of them, but they do an enormous amount of damage."

"Accountant . . ."

Jonah nodded, like a schoolmaster encouraging a pupil who was almost there.

"Are we talking about Brian Todd?"

"That's who we're talking about." He licked his lips as if they had suddenly gone dry. "Can I have that drink now?"

Curle recharged his own glass and poured a stiff measure for the dapper little man who suddenly showed signs of coming apart at the seams.

"Don't think this is easy to do," Jonah said, sipping at his drink so delicately he seemed to be nibbling on the rim of the glass. "Brian is a violent man."

"You think I don't know that?"

They sat looking at one another as if waiting for a knock on the door.

"He's also a successful man," Curle said. He remembered the charity affair at the New Club and Todd swimming, sleek as a seal, in the approval of the great and the good. "I can't believe what you're telling me."

"It's all a façade. Don't you know how much of life is a façade? His own association, the Institute of Chartered Accountants of Scotland, is on to him. They have a regulation and compliance department that's just waiting for the police to make their move, then they'll kick him out. It's all unravelled for him. Just a matter of time. It's been going on for years apparently. I don't know how it started. Maybe a client tempted him to bend the rules. Maybe there was that twisted bit in him and it would have come out anyway. Some people are born to be criminals. They need a lot of luck for it not to happen. Maybe he had bad luck. However it started, it's finished with him up to his neck in crime. Gangsters running security firms, money laundering, financial scams. He's made a lot of money, and society's getting ready to present the bill."

"He told you all this?" It was too much for Curle to take in.

"Christ, of course, he didn't. It's true, though. I told you I'd find out why he hated you."

Bewildered, Curle couldn't see the connection. Some kind of self-protective denial made him stubborn. He said again, "I can't believe what you're telling me."

"Christ!" Jonah blasphemed for the second time. "I sat with Frank Donnelley for three hours last night. He took me all through it."

"Frank Donnelley?"

"You've met him. One time in the office. He's a journalist. He wrote a book about Scottish murder trials and I sold it to Macmillan for him."

"How does he know about Todd?"

"He's a crime journalist. He's been putting this together for more than a year."

"A crime journalist." Curle groped to make the connection. "When Todd told me how Ali had been killed, he said he got it from a journalist he knew. Could it be the same man?"

"I imagine so. Donnelley had been having trouble with his tax, so I introduced him to Todd."

"When was that?"

The knowledge of what he'd admitted moved like a shadow in Jonah's eyes. "Five years ago." He dropped his head and clasped it with both his hands. While doing this, he managed to keep the whisky glass upright, not a drop spilled. Curle couldn't help himself from noting a detail like that automatically. "Brian and I met just after I came back to Edinburgh. We went to bed together the same night."

Like Ali and me, Curle thought.

"What did you mean about finding out why he hated me?" Curle asked.

Jonah looked up. As he did, he must have nudged the glass, for a little of the whisky slopped over the edge.

"Over the years, I told him how things were with you. He's not a man who reads much, but I kept telling him how well you were doing. I remembered how he'd treated you at school. And, of course, he was still a bastard — to me, I mean. It dawned on me gradually that I could — *hurt* him isn't the right word — *get through to him* when I told him how successful you were. Recently, it's really been getting to him. I could see that, though I couldn't fathom why — I knew you weren't making anything like the money he was, and money was what mattered to him. Then he told me he wanted to meet you. I didn't like the idea, but I didn't see any harm in it. How could I know his life was falling apart?"

The old school reunion, Curle thought.

"I told you I'd find out why he hated you, and I have," Jonah said. "There isn't anything else I can do."

"You can tell Meldrum what you've told me."

"The policeman?" He looked horrified. "I can't do that!"

"He won't believe me. He thinks I'm putting up suspects to get myself off the hook."

"Why should I tell him, for God's sake? What would be the point?"

"It would help me."

It wasn't enough. Jonah said more than once that Brian Todd was a violent man. When Curle gave up and they were at the door with the little man on the point of going, Jonah said, "It's taken me twenty-five years, but I've finally chosen between you, Barclay."

260

"That's . . . nice," Curle said. A lord of language, it was the best he could manage.

He was still in the same chair drinking whisky when his family came home. Hearing the car on the gravel, he got up and put the glass still with whisky in it into the cabinet and shut the door. When his wife came into the room, he saw her crinkle her nose as if catching the sweet taint of drink on the air.

"How was it?" he asked.

"He enjoyed himself, except that I wouldn't take him on the Britannia."

"The Royal yacht? Why not? Was it very dear?"

"I didn't even look. I was on the point of doing it — and then I decided, no. I remembered Prince Philip wanted to scuttle it. He didn't want people like us trampling all over it. To hell with him!"

A woman of principle; I'd have taken him on to it, Curle thought. Maybe that's what I'll do. Take him to the pictures and on to the yacht. Show him what a good guy his father is.

CHAPTER
FIFTY-ONE

He was making a statement, sitting at a table with Meldrum on the other side. There was another policeman there too, but it was Meldrum who mattered. During the statement, Meldrum didn't shift his gaze or alter his expression. "When Hetty Logan was murdered," Curle told them, "I was on holiday in Australia. Look, I have the plane tickets here. My son Kerr and I were on Bondi Beach when this terrible thing happened." He was sorry about Hetty Logan who'd lived in the house opposite with her mother when he was a child. The mother had blonde hair and had been abandoned by her husband, and the insurance man when he called said he was never going in her house again because there was human dirt on the floor. Curle was sorry, but he couldn't help being happy because he'd been in Australia when Hetty died. It meant that he could prove he was innocent.

When he opened his eyes, the sun was shining.

"Stop dreaming," Liz said. "The sun's shining."

"I know," he said.

It was slanting in through the gap between the curtains, drawing a line of light down the wall. He was still sleeping on the couch in the study.

262

"Let's do something for Kerr," she said. "Don't be long."

Early sunshine in a changeable month would often be gone by midday, and so they set out to make the most of it while it lasted. The streets were Sunday quiet as they drove through the town. In the Royal Botanic Garden, they walked side by side watching Kerr run through the long shadows thrown by the trees on the grass. They sat on a bench under a cherry tree. The leaves were still small, unfolding like tiny hands. They hadn't spoken for a while. Now he said, "See how they've cut that branch. It must have been growing the wrong way. They don't paint the cut end. They just rub a handful of earth on it. The bacteria in the earth protect it."

"Who told you that?"

"A gardener. One of the times we were here."

"Do you ever come by yourself?" she asked.

"No . . . Do you?"

"Sometimes."

Her reply startled him. Why would she do that? Did she need time to be on her own? What would she think about? He tried to picture her walking the paths by herself.

There were no clouds even by lunchtime, and it seemed the good weather might last all day. It was more comfortable being out and about than going home so they went to the National Gallery of Modern Art and ate lunch in the basement café. Afterwards they looked at paintings till Kerr wearied of it. When they came out, the unclouded sun had warmed the air and there wasn't a breath of wind. The three of them strolled down the long curves of the earth sculpture circling the miniature lake, its water reflecting the blue of the sky. Liz said something and he found himself laughing for the pleasure of the company he was keeping.

As they went into the house, Curle saw an envelope lying behind the door. It was a business envelope, the address scratched out and "Liz" scribbled on it. As he turned it in his hand, he saw that it wasn't even closed. The flap had just been tucked in.

He smiled and handed it to her. "Looks as if it might be from one of the neighbours."

When she slid out the contents, he saw a page ragged at the edges as if it had been torn out of a notebook. She glanced at it and went through into the kitchen.

"Can I go on to the computer, Dad?" Kerr asked. "Till dinner's ready?"

He stood watching as the boy climbed the stairs. On the landing, Kerr turned and seeing him still there gave the thumbs-up sign.

He was still smiling as he went into the kitchen. Liz was standing by the sink looking out at the garden.

"Fall of the Roman Empire," he said.

"What?"

"Or something like that. He's gone up to go on the computer."

He took a beer out of the refrigerator and cracked the tab. As he poured into the glass, he asked, "Was it a neighbour?" When she didn't answer, he said, "That note, was it from a neighbour? I hope it's not a problem with picking Kerr up from school."

When she turned, he saw she was still holding the ragged-edge scrap torn from a notebook. He poured too quickly and set the can and glass on the table.

"Would you look at this, please?" she asked and held it out to him.

Cramped into the narrow space, the letters were square and neat; only the signature sprawled so that it took him a moment to make out that it read Brian.

Hoped to find you in so that I could say this in person. Don't let that husband make you feel guilty. While I was refusing your charms, he was along the corridor with a whore he'd bought. Spanking and fucking her was the way I heard it.

As he looked up, he saw that lager foam was creaming over the rim and beginning to slide down the side of the glass. It seemed to move infinitely slowly, which was one of the effects of shock.

CHAPTER
FIFTY-TWO

"Are you not going to answer it?" the taxi driver asked.

Still watching the house across the road, Curle fumbled with the zip of the inner pocket on his coat. While he was opening it, the noise stopped.

"Just as well," he said. "They scramble your brains."

He switched the phone off, having some superstitious idea that its microwaves might fry his testicles, and put it back in the pocket.

"There's going to be a lot of people with their brains scrambled then," the driver said. "Do you want me to sit here much longer?"

"No!"

There she was, coming out of the gate at the end of the path with a little dog on a leash at her heels.

"Keep the change."

He pushed the twenty-pound note he'd been holding tucked in his palm through the partition and scrambled out of the car.

She was moving surprisingly quickly so that he had to hurry to catch her. From the back she was like a doll or a child, pecking along on very high heels. A beautifully dressed doll, the long coat with the fur collar wrapping her like some prized possession. By the time she emerged from the cul-de-sac, he was almost at her shoulder. "Mrs Todd," he said quietly. She startled, hands flying up as if to protect her face.

"What do you want?"

"To talk to you. If you want, we can go back into your house."

She set off as if she hadn't heard him.

"Fine," he said. "You're going to listen to me. I don't care where."

"Leave me alone," she said. "Brian will be angry."

"Like he was the last time? He's not here though, is he? So you don't have to tell him. Do you tell him everything?"

She veered abruptly off the pavement. It was a main road and he was held waiting for a gap in the traffic, before half running across to the opposite pavement.

"You could have got yourself killed," he said. He could feel his heart pounding. He took deep breaths. "That dog has more sense than you. It doesn't deserve to die."

To his astonishment, she said in a small voice, "I'm sorry."

"For God's sake," he groaned, "don't say that."

Peck, peck, peck, high heels, little bird legs.

"You tell Brian everything," he said. "And you don't have friends any more. And you've lost touch with your relatives."

She stole a glance at him, not saying a word, every doll feature carefully painted.

"He's careful not to hit you on the face," he said.

He didn't know any more if he was looking for revenge or if he was on a mission to save her.

"Let me tell you about Brian."

She stopped and picked up the dog. Holding it close to her, she started off again.

"You can't walk fast enough to get away from this. I'm telling you the truth."

Traffic roared past, but the pavements were empty. It was a road for cars and lorries, not pedestrians. He had harassed her away from her normal circuit for walking the dog.

"Please," she said.

"Brian isn't going to be around for much longer. He's a criminal and the police are going to arrest him. I don't know when, but soon." He looked down at her, but it was as if she hadn't heard. He raised his voice against the surf of traffic heading out of the city towards the Forth Bridge. "Do you understand what I'm saying to you? There's a law now that seizes criminal assets. Maybe that big house will go. You'll be on your own. It's time you thought about yourself."

She stopped and faced him.

"I don't care," she said.

It struck him that she didn't challenge what he'd said. It was possible he was only forcing her to face what she had been denying. In a marriage were there any secrets? Had Liz always known what he was?

"Stand by your man?" Vomit came up into the back of his throat. It was as if he was choking on his own bile. "Are you that stupid? Going to visit him in prison?

Sit in a room somewhere waiting for him to come back?"

"If I have to."

"Why would you do that? Tell me. I haven't had a laugh for a long time."

"I love him."

It didn't make him laugh. He was too full of despair to feel pity. There was nothing more to say. He had said it all, voided it like sickness. And now, bereft of words, it was as if he saw them from the outside, as if he was one of the occupants of a passing car, seeing the two of them on the empty pavement, the little bird-like woman with the dog clasped in her arms confronting the bulk of a man.

"You asked me about my child. I lost it because he beat me. I thought I would die," she said, "but I stood by him. And you think I wouldn't stand by him now?"

In the weeks after his mother's death, his father had walked hours at a time until he was crippled by the growth of bone spurs on his heels. Curle walked like that, trying to find the peace of an exhaustion that would take him beyond thought. When it was almost too late, he remembered Kerr and phoned the neighbour Mrs Anderson to ask if she would keep the boy until Liz came home. By that time, he was sitting in a corner of an empty New Town pub. Later, as the place filled, he came briefly again to his senses and phoned the pharmacy. Not able to face talking to his wife, he left a message for her to collect Kerr when she came home. At some time after that, when the mobile phone, which he had forgotten to switch off, began ringing, he thought it must be Liz. But she would have been home a long time, why would she phone now?

Confused, he had to ask the woman twice to repeat what she was saying before Linda Fleming succeeded in making him understand.

CHAPTER
FIFTY-THREE

The drawn curtains made a mourning light, but they chose not to put on the lamps. When the younger man found the jewellery box, he held it out and shone the torch into it, shaking it gently to stir the contents.

"It's not here."

"I didn't expect it to be."

"Maybe she was buried in it."

"Not according to the undertaker."

After searching the room thoroughly, they started on the rest of the flat. It was almost an hour later that they found the photograph in a box under two others piled at the back of a cupboard. They stood it against a bowl of withered flowers on the dining table and shone the two torches on it.

"Why would she hide it away? You'd think a wedding photograph would be on display."

"Maybe she blamed him for dying," the younger man said. "Is it the one, do you think?"

The older man bent closer. "No way it isn't. But it looks out of place with a wedding dress. I'd guess it's there for a reason. Belonged to her mother, something like that."

"Something old." As explanation, he added. "Like something borrowed, something blue."

The older man grunted.

"And it's not in the flat now. And you think she probably wore it all the time."

"She was wearing it when we questioned her. She kept touching it. Reminded me of the way some people touch wood for luck."

"Luck," the young man said ironically. "Question is, where is it now?"

"With the other necklace," the older man said. "I'd bet my career on it."

CHAPTER
FIFTY-FOUR

"Are you drunk?" Linda Fleming asked.

"It's the only way to travel," Curle said, more cheerfully than he felt.

He staggered slightly, bumping the wall with his shoulder, as he went into the living room. It was a relief to sink into a chair.

"I walked," he said. "I was in a pub in Hanover Street. It's a long walk."

"Have you had anything to eat?"

He thought about it. "I remember breakfast. Must have had something since. Crisps!" He brightened. "Bags of those. Can't remember the flavours."

She muttered something and went out. He dozed and when she came back asked, "Did you swear there?"

Without answering, she laid a tray on the occasional table beside his chair.

"Coffee and ham sandwiches," she said.

"I'm not all that hungry."

"Fuck's sake!" she said. "Eat it."

Shocked, he picked up one of the sandwiches and nibbled a corner off it. She hadn't struck him as a woman who swore. The sandwich tasted good, a little dry; he washed it down with a mouthful of the coffee.

"I don't take sugar," he said.

"It won't do you any harm."

She sat and watched as he worked his way through two of the sandwiches. The others defeated him.

"I'll make more coffee," she said, getting up.

When he'd drunk a second cup, and been out to the lavatory twice, he finally said that he was sorry. "I don't get drunk," he explained. "But you have to admit I'm reliable. I came when you said you needed me." He thought about it. "What did you need me for exactly?"

"I wanted somebody with me," she said. "I think Bobbie Haskell is going to try to kill me tonight."

It didn't sober him at all, or even shock him much, because he didn't believe it for a moment.

He shook his head at her. He spoke slowly, because he wanted her to understand. His main feeling was one of pity. "He isn't the one. We talked about this. Brian Todd killed Ali." He leaned forward confidentially, almost losing his balance. From this angle, he noticed how strong and shapely her legs were. Swimmer's legs. "Thing is," he lowered his voice, "the police are going to arrest him."

"That can't be true." Far from being reassured, she sounded distressed. "How could they make a mistake like that?"

"No mistake."

"How do you know this?"

He puzzled for a moment. "It's true."

"They're going to arrest this man for killing Ali?"

"Ah." Why was everything so complicated? "He's being arrested for something else. But once he's inside, they'll sort it out. You see?"

"Not really."

They sat and looked at one another, as if on two rafts drifting gently apart.

At last, he said, "What do you mean, he's coming down?"

"Sometime tonight. I think he'll wait until the light in the hall goes out."

"Why tonight?"

"I had tea with him this afternoon. I was very relaxed and talkative. Trying to give the impression I liked him. I told him I was leaving tomorrow and that I'd an appointment to see DI Meldrum before I caught my train. And I mentioned the diary as if by accident. Oh, not in so many words, but he'd know what I was thinking of. And at the end I said I'd forgotten my key but it didn't matter, I was always forgetting to lock the door."

"Jesus," Curle said. Even not fully sober, there were so many holes in that he didn't know where to begin. For somewhere to start, he said, "If he thinks you've found evidence in his diary that proves he killed your sister, how the hell could he imagine you liked him?"

"I wish you wouldn't swear," she said. "After I'd done it, I phoned the police. I spoke to DI Meldrum." She bit her lip and looked away.

"What did he say?"

"That I was being very foolish."

"Exactly."

"I wandered about the flat until I couldn't bear it any longer. That's when I phoned you. I didn't want to be here alone."

He sighed. "My wife will be wondering where I am."

She looked at her watch then got up and went out into the hall. When she came back, she stood in the doorway and said, "I've put the light out. I think we should wait in the bedroom."

The moment he stood up, she put off the light in the living room. In the hall, the only illumination came through the half-open door of the bedroom. Not knowing what else to do, he followed her in.

She'd set two chairs almost side by side, halfway between the bed and the dressing table.

"Sit down," she said. "And then I'll put the light out in here."

"We can't sit in the dark!"

"I'll open the curtain first."

As he sat down, he saw she was holding a black stick. It was about a foot long and it had a thick handle resembling the knot where two branches join.

Seeing his glance, she said, "It's a shillelagh. Ali got it on an Irish holiday. It's made of blackthorn. A *hard* wood." She gave the word a vicious emphasis as if smacking it into a skull.

Again he had to fight down the impulse to laugh. Fight it down, because it wasn't funny, none of this was funny. A pathetic woman with God knows what private troubles of her own grieving for her sister, grieving for Ali. How would she cope when she came out of this fantasy? Her tragedy could end in a locked ward.

Keeping it simple, he said, "I doubt if that would be much use against a desperate man."

She studied it and got up again. When she came back, she was carrying a carving knife. He recognised it. A Kitchen Devil; they had one at home.

"You take this," she said, and handed him the blackthorn stick.

When she put the lights out, it was black as a mine. Even when she drew the curtains, it was a matter of shades of black on black. The bedroom was at the back of the house, looking down on to patches of drying green.

He thought about getting up and leaving. He would insist as he went that she locked the door behind him. But how could he be sure that she wouldn't unlock it again? And if she did, what did it matter? There wasn't a chance in the world that anyone was going to come creeping down the stairs. She might in the pathos of her madness sit alone here through all the hours of darkness until the first morning light. As he thought about this, he must have gone to sleep for he woke with her hand probing into his side. He was slumped over, any further and he would have fallen on to the floor. His fist ached from gripping the stick.

When he spoke, his voice sounded rusty from disuse.

He whispered, "Did you say you'd told Meldrum about stealing the diary?"

He thought she wasn't going to answer. Softly at last she said, "I told him it wasn't me who was the thief. I gave Ali a necklace for her twenty-first birthday. I can't find it anywhere."

Although there was no chance of seeing her face, he studied the darkness until his eyes wearied.

He must have slept again, this time slipping into a profound sleep, for he started awake when she touched him. Her hand pressed his arm repeatedly. He opened his mouth to protest, and then he heard the footsteps.

Brian Todd was moving through the hall.

He couldn't conceive of how Todd had come to be there. But for a murderer one night was as good as another. He lurched to his feet and threw the door back. And the monster out of the dark was there, the murderer, the man he hated, it wasn't a dream. With all his force, he swung the stick.

In the instant he felt the impact of wood on bone thrill up his arm all the way to the shoulder, Linda Fleming put on the light.

Meldrum stood there with his right arm hanging by his side. The colour had drained from his face leaving it the colour of soiled paper. With his left hand, he reached out and took the stick, exerting a controlled pressure to loosen Curle's grip on it.

He said quietly, "I've just arrested Robert Haskell for the murders of Ali Fleming and Eva Johanson. Would you like to tell me what you think you've been doing?"

Shakily, Curle sat down on the edge of the bed. Thank Christ, I didn't have the knife, he thought. It was the only thought in his head.

CHAPTER
FIFTY-FIVE

I'm a lucky man, Curle thought, as he sat on the edge of the bed with tears streaming down his face. That morning he had destroyed every note and memento he possessed of Ali Fleming. It had been a cleansing, not just for his sake but hers. He had burned away everything in her which she might have outgrown if she had lived. Let all that remained to memory be the best of her. Out of weakness, he had saved her photograph until last. This image from her past she had given him as a gift. It had been taken looking down on her, so that her face was a triangle and her eyes seemed enormous. "I don't know why you like it so much," she had said. "I seem so needy and desperate."

When Liz came into the bedroom, he was startled. He had thought he was alone in the house.

"My God," she said. "What's wrong?"

He held out the photograph.

She looked at it, then sat beside him.

"Where has this been?" she asked.

"I hid it away. I hid it away with all the others."

"You told me you'd burned them."

"I think I was mad. I've been sitting here looking at it and wondering why you didn't leave me."

"You had them all the time."

"I couldn't bear to burn them. I started to — but then I couldn't."

They sat looking at the photograph of their daughter, who was dead. Liz traced the outline of the child's cheek with her finger.

"Do you know how much I've wanted to look at them? How could you do this?"

"I don't know any more. That's the truth. And once I'd lied about burning them, I didn't know how to tell you. I didn't know how." When she didn't answer, he laid his hand on hers, which lay on the child's cheek. "And yet you didn't leave me."

She wrenched her hand away from under his.

"Understand this. I'm only going to say it once. For Kerr's sake, I won't break up our marriage. I'll never break up our marriage. If that gives you a weapon against me, I can't help it."

They became calmer as the day passed.

In the late afternoon, Kerr was sitting with his mother in the front room doing homework, when Curle brought the photograph downstairs. He sat it on top of the glass-fronted bookcase. When he turned round, they were both watching him.

"This is your sister Mae," he said. "When she died, your mother and I were very sad. But then you came along, and that made us happy." That should have made us happy. "I'm going to leave this photograph here to remind us of her. She'll always be part of our family."

That night he returned from exile in the study. As he lay beside his wife, he felt more at peace than he had done for years. As he was dozing off to sleep, the phone rang.

"Is that you, Curle?"

A man's voice. He didn't recognise it.

Cautiously, he said, "Yes?"

"This is Joe Tilman. I wanted you to know my wife is dead. One of the nurses found her hanging an hour ago. I've just been told."

"I'm sorry," Curle said. His lips felt stiff.

"She couldn't stand being in that place and you were the one who put her there. You killed her, you bastard. I wanted you to be the first to know."

The phone went down and left an echoing silence.

Two hours later, they were both still awake. Curle felt as if he might never sleep again. They had been so separated that he had to explain it all to her, tell her who Martha Tilman had been.

"I can't see that it was your fault," she said for the tenth time. "I don't even know why he phoned. He's just trying to make you feel guilty."

Tilman the negotiator, Curle thought, negotiating another deal.

Later she said, "He's the one who put her in there. Whatever was wrong, it hadn't much to do with you."

Somewhere in the small hours, she said, "You're not a bad man. Whatever you think."

Wearied to the edge of sleep, he swore, "I'll never hurt you again."

He thought she wasn't going to answer, and then thought he heard her say, "I know you mean that," which in the last moment of wakefulness he felt as a judgement and that it was deserved.

CHAPTER
FIFTY-SIX

The day Robert Haskell was given a sentence that meant that he might be back out on the streets in eight years, Curle felt enormously alive and cheerful. Coming out of court, he saw Meldrum standing on his own. Perhaps because of his height, he made an oddly isolated figure.

Going up to him, Curle asked, "Well, was it worth it?"

"McGuigan doesn't think so. He's gone off in a rage."

"Sometimes you have to settle for things as they are." He paused. "I'm sorry about your shoulder. Is it all right?"

"I'm a quick healer. Did you know she'd left the door open? I don't mean unlocked. She'd left it slightly open."

"I thought she'd be at the trial."

"She wrote to me." The big man paused, and it was clear he'd decided to say no more. "Just as well."

On impulse, Curle asked, "Would you care to come for a drink?"

To his surprise, Meldrum accepted the offer.

They walked down the Royal Mile, Meldrum having suggested a tourist pub, as one not likely to be frequented by policemen.

"Where do you usually drink?" Curle asked.

"Wherever I'm not likely to encounter someone I've put away."

"Are there many of those?"

"A fair number over the years," Meldrum said misunderstanding.

"I meant pubs. Morningside ones, eh?" Meldrum laughed at that. "And stay away from the ones in Leith."

"I've got a flat off Leith Walk," Meldrum said.

Even when you weren't a suspect, Curle reflected, the man had a gift for putting you in the wrong.

After they'd found a pub Meldrum approved of, Curle brought the drinks over to the corner table where he'd settled.

"You've heard about Brian Todd?" Meldrum asked.

"No."

"It was on the news. He was found on Calton Hill beaten half to death. At first they thought it was a mugging. He's a homosexual — you knew that?"

"I knew."

"Now there's a suspicion it may have been a warning to keep his mouth shut. He got himself involved with some serious people, not just white-collar crime."

"He is a bastard."

"Likely enough. Just not a murderer."

They sipped in silence.

Curle asked, "When did you suspect Haskell?"

"More or less from the off. He was the obvious suspect. In real life, they're the ones you go for."

"I didn't believe Linda Fleming."

"You're not a detective."

"No," Curle said. "In a crime book, I wouldn't get away with it being the obvious one."

"I'll tell you the strangest thing about it," Meldrum said. "Them all living on the same stair. It was like a domestic."

"I know what you mean. There was that kind of intimacy. People dying in the place where they feel safe." He shook his head. "Even after being in court, I don't understand why he killed Eva Johanson."

"Nobody does."

"I suppose," Curle couldn't help speculating, "he might have turned the anger he felt against Linda Fleming on her. Maybe, with me knowing about the diary, he was afraid to attack Linda. But he had to hurt somebody. There is such a thing as blood lust." He looked to the detective for a response. "Does that make sense?"

Meldrum stared down at his glass, turning it on the table. "There was a lassie in Glasgow two years ago. A prostitute. She was killed the same way, beaten and strangled."

"And you think Haskell might have done it?"

"If he did, there's no way of proving it. Believe me, I tried." He made a little chopping gesture of frustration. "But Eva Johanson should have been enough. That's the one that should have put him away for a long time. It means he'll do it again when he gets out."

"At least you got him."

"Might not be so lucky next time. He might have learned not to take souvenirs from the victims. Want another one?"

"If you've time."

When Meldrum came back, he set the drinks down and said as he took his seat again, "Day like this, it's all you can do. McGuigan'll learn."

"I'd a nasty thought while you were away," Curle said. "Thinking about that prostitute in Glasgow, in my novels the serial killer, Jack's Friend, beats women to death and strangles them."

"I wouldn't worry about it."

Faintly irritated by the dismissal, Curle said, "Haskell worked in a bookshop."

"I'll tell you something about Haskell that didn't come out in the trial," Meldrum said.

"What was that?" Curle leaned forward.

Meldrum gave one of his rare smiles. "Nothing important. That's why the lawyers weren't interested." He took out a notepad and pen and, after writing on it, passed it across. "Haskell had that hidden behind a cupboard door in his bedroom." He had printed in capital letters: THE ENEMY OF LOVE IS DEATH. THE ENEMY OF DEATH IS KNOWLEDGE.

"The lawyers are wrong," Curle said. "Can I keep it?"

"Of course. It's only a bit of paper. He probably stole it from a condom advert. Believe me, murderers aren't interesting."

"How can you say that?"

"They're the rest of us with something missing. It's the people who are able to stop themselves from being murderers who are interesting."

"Like detectives, you mean?"

"If you like."

At that point, relaxed as he'd never thought he would be in the detective's presence, Curle made a mistake.

"Do you remember," he asked, "that note I gave you about Ali Fleming and her Classics Professor?" Meldrum grunted. "Would it be possible to get it back?"

"Why?"

Asked that, Curle found himself embarrassed to explain that he wanted to burn it as he had burned everything else. He was too afraid of seeming pretentious to tell the truth: that he wanted to protect her from the world's ill opinion.

Instead he heard himself muttering, "It might come in useful."

His heart sank as he saw the look on the detective's face.

"That isn't right," Meldrum said.

"I'm a writer," Curle explained, trying for a smile and losing control of it as he felt it slip into a smirk.

The big man contemplated him, rubbing a finger slowly down his jaw.

"You think that's an excuse?" Meldrum asked.

The Lost Gardens

Anthony Eglin

Hidden within the derelict gardens of abandoned Wickersham Priory, a deadly secret is waiting. But when an unsuspecting young Californian named Jamie Gibson finds herself the new owner of the estate — through a surprise bequest from a total stranger — the secret begins to stir.

Jamie, fired with enthusiasm to restore the gardens to their 1930s glory, seeks the help of Lawrence Kingston, a retired professor of botany, eccentric born viveur and amateur sleuth. Lawrence soon unearths an old chapel that leads to an ancient healing well, which yields a human skeleton. As the police pursue their enquiries, Kingston begins his own investigation, following a baffling trail of clues that wind down through the centuries, from the battlegrounds of World War II to the depths of the Middle Ages.

When Kingston finally unlocks the secret of Wickersham Priory, he and Jamie must confront a reckoning that neither of them could have ever imagined.

ISBN 978-0-7531-7720-4 (hb)
ISBN 978-0-7531-7721-1 (pb)

The Mystery Writer

Jessica Mann

It is 1940 and Britain is evacuating its children to keep them "out of harm's way". Ted Johns, son of the groundskeeper at the manor house in Goonzoyle, finds himself in steerage aboard the SS *City of Benares*. Also aboard is the heir to Goonzoyle, Jonathan Hicks. When the ship is torpedoed, the two boys find themselves thrown together, clinging to the wreckage of a life raft. But only one of the boys survives.

In 2003, Jessica Mann researches her new book, Out of Harm's Way — the story of the children evacuated from Britain during WWII. In response to her request for information about survivors of the Benares disaster, she is contacted by Connie, Ted Johns' sister. As Jessica digs deeper, she realises that the events of that fateful night are haunting the present, and when two sets of human bones are found in the grounds of Goonzoyle, the past and present collide.

ISBN 978-0-7531-7620-7 (hb)
ISBN 978-0-7531-7621-4 (pb)